To James

Happy reading

Simon Taylor

Boy and the Wolves of Chylgar

Simon Taylor

For Imogen

Our wonderful
granddaughter

Chapter 1 - The Boy and Gramdi

He was running. Running without tiredness. Running for the joy of it. He was running free.

He needed no shoes and felt the damp earth, the fallen leaves and twigs beneath his bare feet. He felt so light, as though he was hardly touching the ground. The forest seemed endless, but he didn't care. He knew he could run and run. So different from school, where he plodded around the track, always overtaken, always last. No stitch now, no breathlessness. Tonight, he was running free.

His senses felt so alive. He could hear every bird calling and animal moving in the depths of the forest around him. He knew what type of animal had crossed his path, each with its own distinctive scent. Here a deer, there a goat. He wanted to follow each one, track them down. But tonight was for running. He ignored all the tempting smells as he swerved through the trees jumping fallen tree trunks, never slowing, never tiring.

He was thirsty, he would stop at the stream for a drink. He couldn't see it, but smelt and felt its presence ahead. Then he began to hear it. The babbling grew and the forest opened up in the still evening light to reveal a cool misty clearing with the stream in front of him. He paused, instinctively listening for any threatening sounds and then jogged to the water's edge. He didn't cup his hands to gather water, just leaned forward and relished the cool sensation on his face as he gulped it down. It tasted so fresh, so good.

He paused to look around again and then looked down. He froze. His heart raced. There were paws in front of him, not his hands. Long grey furry limbs, not his arms. The reflection in the water, it wasn't him. It was a wolf's face. A wolf's body. He screamed silently and tried to back away, but his limbs felt leaden. He couldn't move. He couldn't take his eyes off the deep yellow and black eyes that looked back at him from the pool. Eyes that seemed to be growing and growing, boring into him.

"Come on son, wake up. It's time to get up and pack. We want to be out today not tomorrow."

His father was looking down at him, smiling.

Boy looked around. This was his bedroom. His desk, his bookcase, yes it was his room. The forest, him running, the wolf's face and eyes; it was a dream but so vivid. He sighed with relief. His father laughed, bent down and ruffled his hair.

"Come and get your breakfast."

He felt groggy as he stumbled out of bed. *Yes, a dream*, he thought. *It must have been a dream.*

It was afternoon and they were on the road. It was cloudy and rainy and that seemed about right. Boy sighed again as he looked out of the car window.

"I still don't see why I have to stay three nights at Gramdi's."

"Because we asked her to," replied his Mum. "It means your Dad and I can go away for the celebration. It's important to us."

"Come on son," said his Dad cheerily. "You know how much she enjoys seeing you. It'll be fun and she will spoil you rotten." He grinned at his son via the rear-view mirror.

Boy glared out of the window. He was eleven and fed up. He sat, arms crossed and spoke to their backs.

"Yeah for an afternoon. But what can I do for three whole days and nights. No phone, no internet, no television, no nothing. Why has she got a thing against me bringing my phone?"

His Mum's tone became exasperated.

"Well you are going and you will have fun, because you always do. You two don't stop talking, do you? You know how she jokes that she wants to see your face not the top of your head and how you can't use your phone and talk at the same time. And you know she always cooks your favourite foods. And anyway," she sighed. "What, just what, is she is going to say about you having decided that you hate your name and won't have it spoken? Honestly! It's beyond me." She tutted, shook her head and stared out of the window.

He shrugged. He hated his name. Always teased about it at school. He had decided three weeks ago, to be called Boy or nothing. After all, that's what he was. A Boy.

As he watched the outskirts of the town slip away and the green fields take over, Boy couldn't help but half-smile. She was right about Gramdi. He knew he would enjoy it, despite the lack of home comforts. But no phone for three whole days? He groaned to himself.

"Look, both of you!" said his Mum, "over there. Look at that dog running across the fields. You know it's so wrong letting your dog run wild like that when there are animals grazing."

"Where?" His dad glanced quickly to his left. "That is a big dog. Never seen one like that. Cross breed of some sort I suppose."

His father slowed the car so his wife could look more closely. Boy watched it running. Loping along, no effort, covering so much ground so quickly. He stopped listening to his parents. His heart quickened. He instinctively knew that it was no dog. He knew exactly what it was. It wasn't a dog, it was a wolf.

At that moment it stopped, turned and looked towards the car. He was sure the black and yellow eyes met his gaze. It was staring at him, looking into him, understanding him. He couldn't look away. He grew icy cold. Those eyes gazing back at him, the eyes of the wolf. It was the wolf in his dreams! But how could it be?

He wanted to shrink away and hide. But before he could think or speak, it suddenly turned and ran into a wood and was gone.

He shook himself and concentrated on his Mum and Dad who were talking excitedly about the celebration, what they would do and who they would meet. Soon they were pulling up outside the old rambling house, his dream and the wolf put to one side.

For over two hundred years the house had stood nestled up against the hill, overlooking the river and town. Boy loved the solid grey stone walls and the tall bay windows that were set either side of the ornate, double front doors. The door frame had a carving of a pack of wolves chasing a deer. He wondered for the first time why it was there, when his thoughts were interrupted by the car stopping.

He tumbled out of the car to be met by an outwardly elderly widow. Shorter than Boy, with white hair tied back in a bun. She was leaning with both hands on her stick looking intently at him. Boy always thought she looked very old, except for the eyes. They shone and sparkled and sometimes when she looked hard, it was as though she was looking through you. He grinned at her and hurried towards her.

After welcomes and hugs they all made their way into the house. All her attention was on Boy, as ever. It made his parents smile as they walked behind him with his weekend bag. Gramdi peppered Boy with questions and listened intently to his answers. Knowing that they would be fine together, his parents hugged him and made their excuses. The journey would be long, they explained and before Boy knew it, he was watching their car disappear down the narrow winding road.

"Well, what shall we do tonight?" asked Gramdi.
He shrugged, he didn't know what to say.

"Well then, I think we should have tea and then wrap up and go out and look at the stars. Tonight, is a special night and has been for countless hundreds of years." She smiled and held up her hand.

"No questions until tonight. Why don't you explore the garden whilst I cook your favourite meal?" She laughed knowing that would bring an immediate smile.

Boy headed out to explore the garden. It was long and seemed to stretch out forever. He walked across the lawn, through a hedge to the back half of the garden, that was just weeds and bushes. The house backed against a hill and as he walked along, the hill base beside him became steeper until at the far end of the garden it was vertical bare rock

He walked alongside it, his fingers tracing the black rock, until there, at the very end of the garden, dug into the rock was the tunnel. Or rather the tunnel entrance. It was set into the hill, about three metres tall and wide. A short distance in, was a wall that blocked the entrance. His feet echoed on the rock floor as he stepped towards it. He was sure the wall was as old as the house itself. The stone blocks were the same grey colour and size of those used to build the house.

There was something about this tunnel. It wasn't that it always felt cold. It was as though there was a story here. A mystery. He never understood his fascination for it. He shrugged, listened and realised Gramdi was calling him. He turned and walked towards the house, suddenly very hungry.

Tea finished and pots washed and put away, Gramdi relaxed in her chair. All the furniture was big and old. His chair was leather and he could hardly touch the floor with his feet. They were playing cards and as usual he was winning. He often wondered if he did win or whether Gramdi let him win. The fire roared and crackled with heat. She felt the cold and always had the house too warm. Boy gave in and took off his jumper. He hated just wearing a short-sleeved t-shirt, but it was too hot and he knew Gramdi didn't care if he was overweight. He just wished he wasn't.

She gasped and stared at the top of his left arm.

"Boy what happened to your arm?" It was still red and a bit sore.

"I did it the other week. Mum was ironing and as I went past, I tripped on something and crashed into the ironing board. The iron fell off and landed on my arm. It did hurt quite a bit."

He twisted his arm so he could inspect it himself. "Mum put a cold press on it straight away. It's okay now, it just left these red marks. Mum thinks they will go soon."

Gramdi kept looking at the marks it had left. The iron had landed face down, the point of the iron towards his elbow. When he looked in the mirror this morning, he thought it was like a face of some sort. Two of the steam holes had left round burn marks, almost like eyes. It was a bit weird. There were other marks below the eyes, but he didn't like to look that closely. Gramdi, was silent and then took his hand. She was staring intently at him, making him squirm a bit. She dropped his hand and nodded at the cards.

"I think it's your turn."

Two hours later and Boy was ready for bed. His eyes felt heavy and he yawned sleepily. Gramdi chuckled to herself and stood up.

"Come on, put on your jumper and coat and let's look at the stars. This is a special night you know. The stars haven't come together in this way for many hundreds of years. It is said that in times gone past, it was thought to be a night of deep magic."

Before Boy could ask what she meant, he was being bustled into the kitchen.

"But Gramdi, it's cold out there and I'm normally in bed by this time."

"I'm sure you are and quite right too, but not tonight. Come on."

The night was cloudless and as soon as they were outside, Gramdi began pointing out the stars, telling him what the constellations were called. She took his arm to lean on and steered them to a path at the back of the house that would lead them up the hill. It started as a gentle slope but gradually got steeper. Boy became aware of Gramdi's laboured breath and the need for frequent stops as they climbed higher.

"Are you sure you want to climb this hill Gramdi? We can go back if you like." He was thinking of his warm bed.

"Young man, I have been walking this hill these past eighty years and more and I am not about to stop now. So, come on, you are slowing us down. I want to get to the stone bench tonight not tomorrow."

"Yes Gramdi. Sorry."

They carried on without speaking. Above them, it was dark but not pitch black. The moon had risen and lit the way in front of them. Gradually the path swung round the side of the hill and when Boy looked back, he could no longer see the old house. They came to a set of old stone steps dug into the hillside.

"We're nearly there Boy, just these steps to go." Gramdi let go of his arm, gathered herself and with a look of grim determination began to climb them. Boy looked around him. Then realised what was unusual. It was the silence. Even at Gramdi's house, there were some sounds: the radio or her bustling around in the kitchen, even the distant traffic noise from the main road. Here though, there was nothing. It hung around him like a cloak. He shivered and trudged up the steps after her.

His legs were aching. He was not used to climbing this far, but he could hardly complain to Gramdi. Soon they were in a semi-circular glade. The ground was flat and looked like it had been cut out of the hillside. In the middle was an old stone bench. It rested on three pillars, each in the shape of an animal sitting upright, but they were so worn it wasn't possible to make out what sort of animal they were. He guessed a dog.

Gramdi slumped onto the bench to rest. She looked up and with a half-smile said,

"There, I told you we could manage!"

Boy sat beside her and smiled back whilst rubbing his legs, which were seriously wobbly.

"So why are we here Gramdi?"

"Soon, Boy soon. Do I have to call you Boy? You have a perfectly good name and it's no use shaking your head at me like that young man. Anyway, we are here to wait and watch and see." And so saying, she reached into her overcoat and pulled out a packet of biscuits and a small bottle of water.

"Come on, help me with these, I think we deserve a small treat after that climb." Boy looked at his watch and was surprised it was already 10:45pm.

"This bench," she looked around, "this whole cut out area, was fashioned and made for this night. Not this night, but for another night centuries ago, when the stars also came together in such a way. This bench would have been for the elders of the tribes. They would have been seated around to the celebrate the time of power."

Her voice drifted away. She sat without moving, then turned and took his hands in hers.

"Before my house was built there was another house and a house before then. For generations our family have lived here and so will you one day. Parent to child, grandparent to grandchild. It has always been the way." She paused and gazed up at the night sky and continued in an excited whisper.

"The moon has gone behind the hill. Now look. Straight in front of you. The two planets. See them? They are its eyes. Now focus on what is around the eyes. The stars, they are forming an outline. The outline of a face. Do you see it Boy? The face of the Wolf!"

Boy stared at the stars. They were just a collection of stars and planets, weren't they? But then he focused on the two planets and gasped. The stars around the planets, they formed the outline of a wolf's head. The eyes seemed to be alive and looking at him and him alone. The head appeared to be growing and growing. He heard a voice. A deep rich voice.

"Take courage child. You are the Prophesy. Follow your heart. It is your time."

He jumped up, looking left and right. But there was no one there.

"What is it Boy? What's the matter?" said Gramdi, reaching for his hand. Boy continued to stare into the dark. There was nothing there.

"I thought I heard a voice. But I couldn't have, could I? Did you hear anything Gramdi?"

She just nodded and whispered,

"No, Boy. I didn't hear anything."

He knew it before she replied. Knew it before he started looking around. The voice. It hadn't been someone speaking in front or behind him. It had been in his head. It was crazy, but it was almost as if it had come from the face in the sky.

Boy thought about the voice. It hadn't been a scary voice. It sounded like someone you looked up to and did as they asked.

Without speaking she stood and together they set off back down the hill.

Gramdi kept her curiosity in check until they were half way down. She glanced at her young companion.

"What did the voice say Boy?"

He frowned, thinking hard.

"I'm sure it said 'Take courage child. Follow your heart. It is your time.' But it said I was the Prophesy. It doesn't make sense does it Gramdi?" He felt rather than saw her looking at him. She leaned close to him.

"Perhaps it does somehow," she whispered. Then almost to herself. "Perhaps it does." She paused to catch her breath, and looked up at the night sky.

"Boy, the stars will form again tomorrow night and as I understand it, for several days thereafter. Perhaps something is to happen during that time. Be careful Boy. Trust your instincts. This is magic you see. Old magic."
She sighed and took his arm.

"I know people scoff and say such things are nonsense. But then there is so much we don't understand. We humans are very arrogant Boy. We like to think we understand everything. There are many things out there beyond our understanding or are yet to be understood."

Boy said nothing. He felt uneasy, scared even, but also excited as though he was at the beginning of an adventure. Just as he was about to speak, they turned a corner and they looked down over the house and garden. Something was wrong. There was a pale almost ghostly light coming from the far end of the house. He couldn't see where its source was. Gramdi stopped.

"I didn't leave a light on did I Boy?"

"No Gramdi, I'm sure you didn't and it doesn't look like a light does it?"

"It's the wrong colour for a fire. It must be a lamp. Perhaps someone is down there. Come on then, let's hurry and see what it is."

As they neared the house they could see that the glow came from the garden. The back end of the garden. They stopped again. At the far end of the lawn, a pale mist was gathering. It rose up and blocked the view of the cliff and the tunnel entrance. They said nothing, but held each other tightly as they moved down the path, past the house and towards the mist. Close to, they could see it was swirling round.

"Gramdi, the light is coming from the tunnel. The mist is coming from there as well. Should we go back to the house?"

"No. I do not sense there is any danger here. It is the night of the wolf. Who knows what could happen. Let's just go to the tunnel edge."

"But what if there is something there. You can't run, can you?" She patted his arm.

"You will have to protect me then won't you." Gramdi chuckled to herself. Boy didn't think it was that funny, but with linked arms they moved slowly towards the mist and the light.

Boy strained his ears to pick up any sound. But there was just the silence of the fog. As they advanced, he noticed that the mist felt strange. It was damp but warm. It was not cold on his face as you would expect on an autumn night. The gentle light grew stronger. It was definitely coming from the tunnel.

As they neared the entrance the light seemed to fade a little, Gramdi gasped and then nodded as if she understood something.

Boy gazed in astonishment looking for the wall that blocked their way. Except it wasn't there. The stone wall had gone. The light shone eerily through the swirling mist coming from deep inside the tunnel.

Gramdi let go his arm and turned to him. She took his face in her hands and looked deeply into his eyes. He wanted to step back, unsettled by her intense scrutiny. He was worried about what she going to say.

"Boy, I do not understand what is happening here. I know it is our destiny to be tied to the night of the wolf. It has been so since time long gone. One day I can tell you more. The voice you heard, the tunnel. Someone or something is calling to you. Boy, I do not sense danger, just a journey. I am too old and frail. Your father is not here. I think it is your time."

He felt excited and frightened. He trusted Gramdi completely, always had. But this.
He gulped and just nodded and turned to face the mist and light. He knew if he stopped or waited a second, he wouldn't do it. He took a step forward and heard her whisper.

"Take courage child." He took more steps and he felt the mist swirl around and enclose him.

Chapter 2 - The Forest of Chylgar

Boy moved forward into the mist, walking slowly, hands in front of him, his eyes and ears alert for any noise or movement. The light was continuing to fade.

"Gramdi," he called out, "the light is going. I'm coming back." No answer. "Gramdi can you hear me?" Silence.

No answer.

He began to feel his stomach churn. The breeze had gone. The mist seemed thicker. He took a few more paces forward and became puzzled and confused. He looked back to see how far he had come in, but the combination of the fading light and increasing mist meant he couldn't be certain where the entrance was. He started to feel really frightened. He put his hand out, searching for the tunnel wall across the tunnel. There was nothing there. The mist was just too thick to see where it and the tunnel were. There wasn't much light left.

Boy looked back, the light was in both directions. He was lost. Too quickly, he turned around, overbalanced and fell onto his hands and knees. Cross with himself, he got up and realised he had no idea which way was in and out. He took a deep breath. He knew he must keep calm and slowly make his way back. His heart was pounding hard. He thought he might be now facing the way towards the entrance and Gramdi's garden. He had to be.

"Gramdi. Gramdi!" This time at the very top of his voice. Nothing. '*Why did she let me come in?*' he thought to himself. '*If I had had my way I would have been in bed and not looking at stupid skies and walking in stupid tunnels.*'

Feeling with his feet he took a few more steps. There was just enough light to see the mist was getting less dense. A breeze on his face told him, he must be near the entrance. He started to relax and carried on slowly walking. Then suddenly, the mist cleared and was gone. He was outside. He looked around him.

"Gramdi. Gramdi! Where are you?" He was irritated that Gramdi must have gone inside and left him to it.

Boy noticed that the moon was high above him now, which was odd. He started to get his night eyes and looked towards the garden and house. But they weren't there. There was grass and then trees. No lawn bushes. He must be confused. A trick of the moonlight. But as his eyes swept around, it was the same. No bushes, no garden, no house. He was surrounded by a tall woodland forest.

He couldn't understand what was happening. If only he had brought a torch! He took more deep breaths and made himself think. He had been walking for quite a few steps, probably more than he realised. Perhaps the tunnel went all the way through the steep part of the hill. After all, he had never climbed it - too steep and high. So, it could be very thin. That was it. He relaxed a bit and turned around to walk back through the tunnel. He stopped in amazement

The tunnel was blocked. Even in the moonlight, he could see there was a wall. He reached out and touched it. It was solid, but not stone. It was wood. Old and snarled horizontal tree trunks that had been carved to form a flat wall.

He gulped a breath in and gritting his teeth pushed with all his might. Nothing. It was solid. It would not move. He looked around wildly, feeling the panic rise up inside him. "Gramdi." He heard his cry swallowed up by the night and knew it was useless.

He had to think. He told himself there must be a reason, an explanation. He double checked the tunnel sides, in case he had come through a side entrance. Solid. So, he was somehow by a forest or wood. There had to be a road somewhere and from a road he could find directions and get to Gramdi's house. Gramdi.

He remembered her words. 'Have courage child'. His heart pounding, he resolved to go on. The moon seemed closer and brighter than normal, it looked different somehow. He shook his head. He had some light, which was a bonus. If only he had brought a torch.

Boy knew he had to focus. The moon was in front of him. So, if he walked facing the moon, he couldn't walk in a circle. The wood seemed to be of tall trees. Not pine trees, in fact not like any he had seen before. There didn't seem to be much undergrowth. Pockets of bushes that were as tall, no taller, than him, but lots of clear space as well.

He set off. At least he was warm and had proper shoes. The grass felt springy underfoot. Walking calmed him and he became less scared and more excited. He undid his coat. Actually, that was a bit strange too, he thought. He wondered why it had become so warm, after all it was autumn. He was sure it wasn't like this half an hour ago.

The floor of the wood was pretty flat with just gentle undulations. The moon shone through the trees, giving Boy enough light to see where he was going. The moon was still ahead so he knew he was keeping a straight line. It was quiet though. Not a sound, as though the whole wood was asleep, just his feet walking through the leaves and the occasional snap as he stepped on a twig.

After a few minutes, he began to wonder how big the wood was. What if it was a forest? He shook his head. There were no big forests by Gramdi. He was sure it was open land and woods, small woods. He would be fine he told himself. As long as he didn't panic. He just had to keep going straight, he told himself, hoping it was not too far.

A rustle. In the trees to his left. He was sure he heard a rustle. Boy instinctively knelt down beside a bush, so he couldn't easily be seen. He peered through the leaves. He strained to see or hear what had made the noise. He didn't see anything at first but then there were shapes moving towards him. Big shapes. Animals. He sighed with relief, they were deer!

He had never seen deer like this before though. He didn't even know deer lived near here. The lead one was as big as a horse, with two very long and very sharp looking horns. There were about twenty of them, including mothers and fawns.

Suddenly the leader stopped. He looked directly at the bush where Boy was hiding. He hadn't moved? Had he?

They all stopped. All seemed to be staring at where he was hiding. As one, they suddenly darted away and were gone.

Boy was about to get up when he heard another noise. This time it came from behind him. Was it him the deer had been looking at or was there something else, more dangerous that had spooked them? His knees were beginning to ache, but he daren't get up. Very slowly he started to twist round so he could see what was coming towards him.

The noise had stopped. There it was again, almost like whispering. The quiet rustling again, then nothing.

A shape. He could see a shape, no two shapes. They were coming in his direction. They were humans. He breathed a sigh of relief. They were taking great care as they continued to slowly walk towards him. He didn't know if they had seen him. They were taller than him but not much and they were talking.

"Well they must have heard you. I wasn't moving when they stopped. Some hunter you are going to make!" It sounded like a girl's voice.

"Could have been something else. An animal."
Definitely a boy.

"I suppose it could have been either of us," she replied good-naturedly.

Their accents were very strange, definitely not local. But they obviously knew the area and could tell him the way home. Smiling and relieved, he was about to stand up when they came into view. He stopped instantly, eyes wide, mouth open. At the same time they spotted him, grabbed each other and stood still gaping.

Chapter 3 - The Kith of Chylgar

The moon was so bright, he could vaguely make out what they were wearing. Both wore tunics and leggings of some sort. They were carrying spears.

"Look at his clothing," the girl whispered. "Where are you from? Can you understand?"

"Careful Mellana," said the taller one nervously, "he's crouching," he aimed the point of his spear at Boy. "Could be dangerous."

Boy's knees were screaming and he knew he had to stand and show he wasn't dangerous. He slowly got up, hands in front of him, palms open, to show he meant no harm.

The girl leaned forward, put her hand on the tip of the boy's spear and lowered it.

"He means us no harm Detra." She smiled and stepped towards him. "Stranger, do you understand me? What Kith are you? For you are not from here, are you?"

"Hello! Do you understand!" Detra said loudly.

Mellana looked skyward and shook her head.

"I'm sure he's not deaf. But I will be if you shout like that again and you will scare every creature within a day's run."

Detra winced.

"I'm Mellana and this is Detra," the girl said encouragingly.

Boy stuttered, "I'm Boy. Where am I? I'm lost. I came through the tunnel. I need to get back to the other side of the hill."

They looked at each other, then at Boy. Detra spoke.

"What do mean you came through the tunnel? How could you? It's blocked up. Anyway, it is forbidden to enter, it always has been."

Then a thought came to him. "Are you alone or are you with others?" and so saying both of them raised their spears and began looking around them.

"No, no," Boy said quickly and put his hands out again. "I'm alone. I was visiting my Gramdi. She lives in the old farmhouse on the other side of the hill. I came through the tunnel by mistake and when I tried to go back it was blocked. I don't know where I am, but I need to get back before I'm missed. So, can you tell me the way to the nearest road to take me round the hill, so I can get back home?"

Detra and Mellana looked at each other. It was clear they didn't understand what he was talking about.

Mellana spoke first.

"We are the Kith of Chylgar. All this, to the mountains of the North, is the land of the Chylgar and always has been. What is a 'gramdi' and 'road'? How can you have come to us by the Gateway? You said it was blocked, as it always has been." She looked doubtfully at him again.

Boy started to worry. "I'm telling the truth, honestly. Please just show me the way to the nearest road, I mean path and I'll leave you alone."

Boy just felt this was crazy. The sooner he was gone from the two children the better.

"I don't know this area. I don't know a town called Chylgar or a family called Kith. So, if you could show me a path out of here, then I'll be on my way."

"But there is no such path. The forest reaches up to the mountains. You cannot go around or across them. This is the end of Chylgar. No one has ever crossed the mountains."

They had been stepping closer to each other and were now face to face. Each could see the honesty in the other's eyes.

Mellana touched Boy's coat. "Your clothing is so strange."

Boy nodded in agreement for he now realised their tops and long shorts appeared to be made of giant leaves and leather. Not like anything he had ever seen.

"Your story makes no sense," Mellana said. "Yet you believe you are telling us the truth. I cannot see what to do, other than take you back to our people. Centra our Leader, will decide what should happen."

Detra nodded in agreement, but Boy knew he had to get back and soon.

He was about to protest, when the children as one, dropped to the floor and pulled Boy down with them. They signalled him to be silent and still. He strained to see what had alarmed them. Then he saw it, a large grey shape between the trees. Now there were two. No three. Then as they grew in number, he realised what they were. Wolves. But not the wolves he had seen at the zoo. These were bigger, much bigger. In fact, huge. Long legged, with grey and black fur. He couldn't move. He was frozen to the spot.

He became aware of the two children getting up, pushing him to his feet so he stood between them. They raised their spears facing the pack of wolves. Boy felt they were trying to protect him and knew he must somehow follow their example and try and show no fear. But he was afraid. So afraid.

Boy thought there must be eight or ten wolves in total. He watched the lead wolf almost amble towards them and then stop about fifteen metres away. The other wolves formed a semi-circle around them.

They were so huge, there was no way the children could protect him. He licked his dry lips, felt his heart pounding. The children were pointing the spears at one then another wolf, as though by doing so it was somehow holding them back.

The three of them started to back away. The wolves took a step forward. Another step back by the children, another forward by the wolves. The ritual continued.

"What are they doing here?" Mellana hissed. "I have heard tell of them, but never seen them before. They live in the North. Wait. We are being herded," she said. "I don't know why, but we are being pushed away from the village."

The children continued to back up, the wolves gently nudging them towards the edge of the wood. Then they were out of it and on the field in front of the tunnel.

"What do we do Mellana?" Detra looked around. "We are being pushed towards the Gateway wall. What are we to do then?"

They were half way across the grass, when the pack leader stopped and looked around at the other wolves. They stopped at the lead wolf's command and sat down on their haunches. The children kept backing up until they were in front of the tunnel entrance. The wolves made no move towards them.

Boy did not know what any of this meant. "Why have they stopped. What are they going to do?" he asked.

"I don't know. We wait I suppose," said Detra, "and hope they come from the village to find us."

Boy was drawn to the lead wolf. It seemed to be looking at him intently. He didn't want to look into its eyes, but felt as though he had to. He couldn't help himself. He lifted his head, and gazed into its black and yellow eyes. He instantly felt the fear drain from him and a calmness sweep around and into him. They weren't going to kill them. He knew that they were safe. He took a step forward. The girl grabbed his arm.

"Boy," she hissed, "what are you doing? Stay behind us."

He turned to look at her, smiled and released her hand.

"It's okay. I'm sure." He turned back to face the wolf. It stood up and seemed to be studying him

Boy gulped. It was so big. It had to be two metres tall. He generally didn't like dogs, never mind wolves, so why he was doing this he had no idea. Another step forward. Yes, he would be fine. Two of the other wolves growled, bared their teeth and began to move towards him. Their leader turned to look at them and snarled. They both dropped their heads and ears, and quickly returned to their position.

"Be careful Boy," Detra whispered.

Slowly and step by step he walked towards the wolf. It held his gaze the whole time. Boy felt it was as though it was making up its mind. He stopped, so close now. A thought appeared to Boy. It was like a voice. A rich deep voice in his head.

"*Yes, you are the one. Your time is nearly upon you. Do not delay your return. Time presses upon us.*"

The wolf then turned away and followed by the rest of the pack, loped gently back into the trees. Boy stood stock still. Did he imagine the voice? It was the same voice he'd heard before, when gazing up at the stars with Gramdi. Wasn't it? Could wolves talk in this strange place?

His confusion was interrupted by Detra slapping him on the back, full of admiration.

"I don't know what happened there, I could never have done that." He regarded Boy curiously. "Who are you?"

The girl turned Boy around, gently smiled at him and said quietly.

"I think we owe you our lives. Thank you. What can we do to repay you?"

Boy smiled back warmly. He had never been treated like this before in his life. He didn't know what to say. He couldn't mention the voice, he didn't understand it himself.

Mellana gestured towards the tunnel entrance and the rows of logs blocking it.

"Is this how you came into Chylgar?" Boy nodded.

"So how did you walk through the wall then?" asked Detra.

Boy shrugged. "It wasn't there, the tunnel was full of mist. I just walked through, I thought I was going back to

Gramdi's garden. But when I came out and looked back the wooden wall was there."

He walked up to it and ran his fingers along the rough, time-worn wood. Suddenly he stiffened.

"It can't be can it?" He said aloud. The wood was softening under his touch. He pushed against it and felt his arm go through. He pulled it back with a cry.

The two children grabbed each other in wonder.

"Are you a Seer?" asked Detra.

Boy shook his head. "No, no. I'm just a boy. I don't understand what is happening." He took a deep breath and tested the wall again. His hand went through and returned undamaged. "But I think I have to go back tonight, somehow through this wall."

"Will we see you again?" asked Mellana.

Boy didn't know what to say. It was all too confusing. He surprised himself by answering, "Yes, I think so."

He couldn't think of anything else to say.

"Goodbye and-" he shrugged his shoulders, half-smiled and turned to face the wall again.

They both watched him.

"Be careful," they whispered.

Boy took a deep breath and pushed against the solid old oak beams. As before, his hand went straight through. It felt damp and stringy, as though the wood had turned into a wall of fog and cobwebs. He shut his eyes tight and grimaced, but he kept pushing. Then he was through. The cobwebs had gone. He opened his eyes.

He was in the tunnel, mist swirling about him. There was a light ahead. He put his arms out, waving them from side to side until he felt the wall. Step by step he moved forward taking comfort from the feel of the rough stone tunnel against his fingers. The mist grew less dense and the light started to dim. He hurried on, the light weakening with every step. It died. He could see nothing, feel nothing.

He stopped. But at that moment, he felt the cold autumn wind against his face. He had to be nearly through. A few more paces and he began to make out the outline of the tunnel entrance. He carried on and grinned as in the moonlight, he could see the familiar outline of the garden and beyond it the welcoming sight of the old farm house.

Boy ran all the way through the garden and burst through the kitchen door to see a pleased and expectant Gramdi, sitting patiently in her chair.

"Gramdi, you will never believe what happened, I went through the tunnel and it wasn't our world, don't know where it was but the children looked so different and the Wolf was huge!" At which point he ran out of breath and Gramdi laughed and stood up and hugged him. She wanted to know everything from start to finish, whilst she made him a hot chocolate drink and opened the cookie jar, she kept especially for him.

He told her about finding himself in the strange land and how he met the children of Kith. He stood and put his hands out wide when he described the wolves and their size and about walking towards them. His eyes sparkled and were full amazement at his own daring.

He revelled in Gramdi's smiles of encouragement, her periodic gasps but did not notice her looks of concentration and thoughtfulness. Then he reached the part of the story where the wolf spoke to him in his head. He hesitated conscious of how strange it would sound.

Gramdi leaned forward, took his hand between hers and smiled up at him.

"Go on Boy. What happened when you faced the big wolf. You can tell me what he said, no matter how silly it may sound."

Boy looked up sharply. "You know! You know about the voice in my head? That he, the wolf spoke to me."

"No, I didn't know, but I guessed." Gramdi patted his hand. "A tale for another day. Go on," she said encouragingly.

Now more subdued and unsure of himself Boy described the wolf and his rich deep voice. A voice he knew he never heard in his life before. It was dawn by the time he had finished. Whilst he sat contentedly munching a biscuit, Gramdi sat back reflecting.

"Boy, the last time you were here, your Mum was telling me about the big dog that lived next door. About how aggressive it could be towards strangers, though not with you. But she never got to finish the story."

"Rocky? I think he must be a cross of every big breed," he laughed. "I don't know why they took it in. Mum thought they were mad to do it. It barks all the time and it has to be locked up when there are visitors, but when I go around, he stops and wags his tail. He puts his head on my lap and just looks up at me. He's strange, but I like him."

Gramdi nodded thoughtfully.

"I'm glad you like animals. Always remember Boy, and it's something I always follow, no matter how big or ferocious an animal is, show strength and show courage. Will you remember that?"

Boy nodded, not really understanding why she was saying it.

"I do believe you Boy, about the voice in your head, the wolf's voice. It must have been very exciting and very confusing. Perhaps this can't be solved now, perhaps we just have to wait and see. For now, I think your whole adventure had best be our secret, don't you?" Boy agreed immediately. He had dreaded telling his parents. He just knew they wouldn't understand. Gramdi looked outside, it was light.

"Time for bed I think, don't you?"

Boy suddenly realised how tired he was. Without another word, he slowly climbed the stairs and without even getting undressed, collapsed onto the bed and fell into a dreamless sleep.

It was the smell of food that woke him up. At 3pm! He felt warm and comfortable but the smell of food was too much. He leapt out of bed and rushed downstairs to be greeted by a smiling Gramdi and a plate piled high with his favourite food. For the next few minutes there was silence apart from the sound of cutlery on plate and the occasional "hhmmm" from Boy.

"Thank you Gramdi, that was the best breakfast ever! Or lunch or whatever that was." They both laughed.

Later that evening Gramdi sat Boy down at the table and took his hands.

"There will be a Wolf sky again tonight. I do not know why the Wolf sent you back last night, other than to ready yourself for the journey. I think their land needs you Boy. Does that make sense to you?"

Boy thought long and hard. He thought about his dream. About when he was in the car and saw the wolf running in the field, then stopping and looking at him. He thought about the wolf sky. About being in Chylgar and walking towards the wolf without fear.

He thought about the wolf's voice telling him it was his time. His time? Time for what? He was just Boy after all. He was no hero. He wasn't in anyone's group. Not good at sport, okay at school work, just okay at everything really. He was just Boy.

Then he remembered the thrill and power when he ran in the dream. The confidence, the calm and yes, excitement all rolled into one, when he walked towards the wolf in Chylgar. The admiration in the faces of Detra and Mellana. He was nervous, scared really, at the thought of going back, but how could deny that voice. He had to return to Chylgar.

"Yes, Gramdi I'm ready now. I'm ready to go back if the tunnel is open for me."
She nodded and half-smiled. She seemed to understand and accept so much.

"Gramdi, have you been to Chylgar?"

She laughed and started to bustle about.

"Have I been there? What a question. Come on, you need to get ready."

Boy was suddenly nervous. It was getting dark. Going back had seemed such a good idea in the daylight. He went to the window to see if the tunnel was lit.

At first the garden looked dark. Then he could dimly see it, a very dim pale light had come on somewhere. He kept staring, it was getting brighter. He could make out the outline of the tunnel clearly now. He watched, as the light grew and the mist began to seep out of the tunnel, swirling around.

"Gramdi, the tunnel, it's lit up. It must mean the wall has gone." He stopped, and looking at Gramdi, felt his stomach tightening. It meant he could go back.

Gramdi hugged him then held at arm's length.

"Boy, I do not know the future, but I feel the old magic. It is here and around you. You are a chosen one Boy. Be strong and you will be safe. I am sure."

Boy just nodded. He felt confused by her talk about 'chosen one' and 'old magic'. But, he knew he couldn't stay any longer. He had to go now or he never would.

He hugged her in return, put on his coat and stepped out into the cool air.

Chapter 4 - The Tunnel

Boy walked slowly towards the mist and light. He felt the mist envelope him with its damp fingers. As he entered the tunnel, the light dimmed and within a few paces it had gone. He felt for the wall and shuffled along, one arm in front of him and the other tracing the rough rock. A torch! He had forgotten to bring a torch again.

This time it felt like an age, but gradually the light grew brighter. The mist began to clear and he stepped out into daylight. It made no sense because the sun was shining. The clearing and wood were in front of him as before, but now, instead of seeing them dimly in moonlight he could see everything. He turned around to better see the tunnel entrance. It was set into a hill and above it, rising steeply were snow covered mountains. No wonder Detra had said he couldn't go around them.

The wood, it was big, it was a forest. It was different from home. The trees were all different. Each one was made up of several trunks that wound round each other. The leaves were quite small, so you could see into the forest. In the far distance beyond the treetops he could see the outline of mountains, almost blue in colour.

Boy decided he would go to the village to find his friends. He set off into the forest, noting where the sun was. He hoped it would lead him in the right direction. It was hot, he had already taken off his coat and knew he would soon have to take off his jumper. *It has to be summer here* he thought.

The forest was full of bird song. He looked up to see a flash of yellow and bright green and then it was gone. In the distance, he could hear a noise, the movement of a large animal. He concentrated on it and then relaxed as it seemed to be going away from him. He wondered if he would see any deer again. All the time he was watching for signs of his friends and the wolf.

There was nothing scary so far, the forest was wasn't densely wooded and there were big leafy bushes scattered around the forest floor. The sun poured through the tree canopy and he could see a long way in front of him.

"Do not move if wish to live."

Boy froze terrified. He gasped as four shapes rose up from the forest floor. They were men, men holding spears pointed at him.

"Who are you that walks in our lands?"

They were tall, short-haired, no, their hair was tied behind their heads. They had dark skin and wore the clothing Detra had worn. Tunics and leggings made of leathery type leaves. Thin shoes, that again looked leaf-like. The one who had spoken was looking around him.

"Where are the others. Who do you travel with?"

Boy spluttered out, "I am alone. I came through the tunnel. I met Detra and Mellana last time and I have come back to find them."

The others lowered their spears, they had heard about him. The leader still looked angry and kept his spear firmly pointed at Boy.

"Why should we believe that you have travelled alone. If this is a trick and there are others, you will pay for deceiving us."

"Gracha, he is exactly as Detra said. He saved their lives remember. We owe him our thanks." The speaker gave Boy a wide grin and turning to Gracha, placed his hand on the others spear, gently lowering it.

"You are too trusting Luntra, but you always were," snarled Gracha. He turned on his heel and walked away, looking left to right for strangers.

Luntra approached Boy.

"I am Luntra and we will take you back to our village. We owe you our thanks and there is much to learn about you I think." He smiled down at Boy,

"Thank you," was all he could think of to say.

As they walked Luntra introduced the others and explained that they were out hunting. His two other companions introduced themselves and started to pick up shoulder bags that had been hidden in the bushes.

"Why don't you three continue the hunt and I will take the boy back to the village?" With a wave and a wish of good luck they disappeared into the undergrowth. Luntra put his hand on Boy's shoulder and guided him to a narrow path.

"It is not long to our village. I would like to hear of your journey, but you will be asked by our leaders and telling your story once will be more than enough I am sure."

Boy felt very relieved and quite excited. He was sure this man would help him. They walked in silence through the forest until Boy could not resist saying.

"Your world is different to mine. I have never seen trees or bushes like this."

Luntra nodded and went on explain what the different varieties were. Time quickly passed and soon they reached the forest edge. There before them were green rolling hills but what caught Boy's eye was the broad river beneath them, and scattered along the riverbank were wooden two-story houses. As they walked down, he realised the roofs which seemed to be made of a thick shiny material, were actually layers of giant leaves, sewn together somehow.

In the village people were busy walking between huts. Some had open sides and appeared to be shops. The ground was hard earth. The people started to be aware of Luntra and himself. He supposed it was his strange clothing. Their bustling and conversations halted as they passed. More and more people stopped and stared. Then questions to Luntra about who the child was and whether he was taking him to the council. Luntra was a man of few words and either nodded or just replied, "As is fitting."
He pointed to a large building in front of them.

"I will take you to meet the council and they can decide what should happen."

Boy was about to ask what he meant when he heard a familiar voice.

"Boy it's us, Detra and Mellana. What are you doing here?" Grinning and running towards him were the two children. They put their hands on his shoulders and then continued to walk with him.

Detra was eager for information.

"When did you come back? Are you hungry? Are you going to the council? We went there with our Mums and Dads. We told them about you and about how you stood up to the wolf. We've never been to the Council before, it was quite scary. You see."

"Detra," protested Mellana. "Enough questions and chatter about the Council."

Luntra laughed. "Mellana is right, you will wear him out with your questions. Yes, we are going to the Council and yes, he will have food and drink and yes, they will know again of his courage," he stopped and then smiled. "For you will come with us and remind them."

Detra and Mellana looked at each other with a mixture of pleasure and nervousness. Boy realised it must be a big event to meet the Council. He was about to ask about the Council when Luntra pointed out a big building at the far end of the village.

Taller than any of the houses, its 'V' shaped roof was supported by huge vertical logs. Each log was carved with symbols and animals. Around the entrance a giant wooden frame again covered in carvings, from the bottom of the left corner all the way up and round and to the bottom right corner, was of a wolf pack running.

Boy just stared at it, for It was just like the carving around Gramdi's front door. He was sure it was identical, just bigger. Then he stopped and gasped, for at the centre, above the middle of the frame was a face. A face he had seen in his dream and on his first visit. It was the face of a wolf.

"Yes, it is a wolf," whispered Mellana. "Just like the wolves you saw."

"We will learn more inside. Come," said Luntra as he eased the three of them forward.

They walked into a large open auditorium. Seats were set out in a semi-circle facing a raised platform, on which was a 'V' shape table. There sat a group of men and women. All were in the same type of leafy tunic. Except one. She was very old, her tunic was grey and black, the colours of a wolf in fact. He realised her chair was higher than the others and the wooden back appeared to be carved not plain. The man at the centre of the 'V' looked up.

"You are ever welcome Luntra." He leaned back and stared at Boy making him very uncomfortable. He hated being looked at. What made it worse was he was sweating. It was so warm in the hall and he was so hot in his jumper. The man gestured towards Boy. "Is this the child that was spoken of?"

"It is the one, Centra, the stranger from another land who stood proud before the wolf. His name is Boy." Luntra gently nudged Boy forward.

Centra leaned forward, "Come closer. We have heard of your bravery Boy." Centra studied him, "Tell us, where are you from and how did you come into our lands?"

"Where is your hospitality Centra. I am Wolfrea. I am the Seer of Chylgar," said the old woman as she stood. She was only short and leaned on a heavy stick. Her eyes smiled and she reminded Boy of Gramdi.

"Do you not see. The boy is hot and tired. Let him sit and bring him water and food." She waved her hand at Boy. "Put down your coat and," in a puzzled tone, "take off your other coat. It is winter in your land isn't it."

Suddenly there was shouting outside and a man, rushed in breathing heavily.

"The wolves. They have returned. They are here."

Behind the man followed villagers all demanding to know what had happened and what was to be done. Boy could see the fear and confusion on their faces. All too quickly the hall was full. The noise was deafening.

"Calm. We need calm." Centra shouted, arms outstretched, commanding attention. He sat and signalled all around him to do the same.

"Bring him water," he ordered and turning to the messenger signalled for him to begin.

The man spoke breathlessly, Boy could see he was scared. He didn't really understand, because he had not felt afraid when he had met the wolves.

"I was on the hill, west of the village and saw them in the distance. There were ten of them, running towards me. I ran and they followed, but made no effort to catch me. They have stopped. They are just sitting, as though waiting for something."

The villagers all started talking again and Centra again called for order. It was so hot in the room, Boy decided he could slip his jumper off. He immediately felt better and listened as Centra called for his hunters to gather with their spears on the outskirts of the village.

"*We are here for you, child.*"

Boy instantly froze. Centra and villagers were still talking. They had not heard it. But Boy had. He knew that voice. He looked up and saw Wolfrea looking around, a puzzled expression on her face. She caught Boy's eye and looked deeply at him. The voice spoke again.

"*Come to us. It is your time.*"

He looked away, but his eyes were drawn back to Wolfrea. She was still staring at him. She slowly rose and cried out.

"Quiet everyone. There is more here than a messenger to consider. Centra, let the Council meet in private. The children should stay. I think the boy's arrival now is of great import."

The room went quiet, everyone was staring at him. Boy felt himself going red with embarrassment. He studied the floor, but knew he had to look up at her. The old woman whose eyes were full of questions.

Centra spoke again, his voice clear and full of authority.

"As Wolfrea has spoken. Let everyone wait outside. Quickly, clear the hall. There is no time to waste."

Boy heard murmurs of discontent. The villagers clearly wanted to know more but gradually left the room. Only the council members, two guards, Luntra and the children remained. They all moved to the front. Boy glanced at Mellana and Detra. They half-smiled at each other. He saw in their faces the mixture of puzzlement and excitement and a bit of the fear that he felt.

Centra sat down and looked questioningly at the Seer.

"What is it you sense Wolfrea?"

She continued to focus on Boy. She walked around the table and down the steps at the side. All the time her gaze was on him.

"You heard him too, didn't you Boy. It was you the wolf was talking to wasn't it?" The council members and children gasped as one.

"What voice?" Questioned Centra.

Wolfrea held up her hand for quiet.

"You are the reason that the wolves have come."

Boy looked at his feet and just nodded. There was a knot in his stomach.

"Did he speak to you the first time you came?" Again, he nodded.

"What did he say, can you remember?"

Boy was reluctant to repeat what the Wolf had said.

"It may be important, don't be frightened," she said in a gentle voice.

He looked up and felt reassured by her smile.

"He said my time had nearly come and I shouldn't delay coming back. That's why I came back, because Gramdi - my Grandmother, thought it meant I was needed here. That's why I came back. I meant no harm."

She smiled and patted his shoulder.

"You are not in trouble child. I am the only one in the land who can hear the voice of the wolf."

She looked around. "The wolf can speak. The Seer of the Kith can hear him. This is as it has always been. You know this. It spoke just now. It said, 'Come to us, it is your time.' But it was not spoken to me, was it Boy? It seems I am not only one who can hear the wolf."

They all stared at Boy. Although he felt uncomfortable, a bit of him liked it really.

"Is this why they are here? The wolf pack have never gathered like this, or visited our village," commented Centra. "Do you think our people are in any danger?"

She faced Centra. "I do not think they mean us hurt. They are here for the child. But why? Why have they called you Boy?"

She turned back and stood directly in front of Boy, reached out to pat his shoulder again, but stopped and gasped. She nodded to herself and smiled at him. She traced the scar on his arm with her fingers.

"Now I understand. You are he."
She turned to council. "His arm. It bares the mark. The mark of the wolf. I know for sure. It is part of the Prophesy."

The others looked puzzled. Centra started to speak when Wolfrea put out her hands and intoned,

"Yet only one on two legs can help you, and only he who carries our sign." The others looked bemused.

"It is the Prophesy of the wolf packs that has been passed from generation to generation. It is also passed from Seer to Seer. The wolves must be in grave danger. Come, quickly, we must meet them and now."

Centra stood. "Wolfrea, I don't understand all that is happening, but I know to follow your instincts. We will go to meet the wolves."

Chapter 5 - The Wolf Pack

"Give me your arm for support young man." Wolfrea and Boy followed Centra out of the hall. The children and other members of the council followed behind them. The villagers had formed a large semi-circle around the doorway. They stood aside to let the group pass.

Boy felt bewildered. What did Wolfrea mean about being a chosen one? What was he supposed to do? He knew he was no hero or fighter and panic started to rise up within him. What would happen if he was supposed to do something or know something and he failed?

His head swirled with thoughts as they passed the houses and shops and made their way towards the fields beyond.

As they left the village, a couple of hundred of metres or so in front of them sat the Wolves. There were ten of them. They sat on their haunches. The wolves formed an arrow shape behind their leader.

The Wolves rose as the group approached. The same deep, rich voice spoke to Boy in his head.

"*Come, we mean you no harm.*"

Wolfrea heard it too. She nodded and told the others.

Centra instructed the villagers and warriors to halt whilst the Council and children continued forward.

Close to, Boy could feel the power of the wolf. Yes, it was taller than him, taller than the adults in fact. He could see the strength in the long legs and muscled body. But it was its face and eyes. The yellow and black eyes. They were somehow commanding, solemn, full of knowledge and authority. He couldn't look away.

The wolf released Boy's gaze and surveyed the gathering villagers. It turned to Wolfrea.

"We salute you Wolfrea, Seer of the Kith of Chylgar. We salute you Centra, Leader of the Kith. We come here in peace. We are on a journey to save our packs and your people, a journey that has been foretold. I would have us talk of what has happened and what must happen to save us all."

He looked at Boy. Then back at Wolfrea who was explaining to Centra and the villagers what was being said.

Centra stood thinking for a moment and then spoke to the villagers.

"Let all gather behind us. Let the pack be welcomed. Bring water and meat. We will sit and take council on this." Then nodding in salute to each of the wolves, he continued. "You are bid welcome to our village. Holding out his hands, he signalled everyone to sit down on the lush grass.

Boy looked around and seeing everyone else settle on the grass, followed suit. He was pleased to see that Detra and Mellana had somehow managed to sit just behind him. He felt reassured when they gripped his shoulders in support.

The Voice began again, and he heard Wolfrea speaking the Voice's words at the same time, so all the village could know what was being said.

"My name is Wolvzzar. I am the leader of our pack and chosen by all the packs to lead the Clan. Since the Time of the Ravages, when man and wolf last came together to fight the soldiers of the Emperor from over the mountains, we have lived in peace. You and the four villages on the plains in the South, and we, the five packs that form the Clan of the forests and mountains of the North.

In return for your help then, we have protected the plains from the creatures that would pass through from the mountains. The creatures of the Empire that would kill and destroy all that live here. This you know. But for four summers past, soldiers have been seen again. Soldiers of the Empire. We think they have somehow tunnelled through the very mountain itself. We did not kill them, but turned them back, so that they would know the Empire is not welcome.

"This spring and summer a sickness has developed amongst our Clan. All the packs have been so affected and now there are too few left to protect our land."

The wolf ceased for a moment to allow Wolfrea to finish repeating his words. He looked at all the villagers before continuing.

"The packs came together at a Council. The words of the Prophesy handed down to each pack leader since before the Time of the Ravages were spoken."

Boy listened in awe as the Voice began to intone the Prophesy. At the same time Wolfrea spoke it out loud.

> '*When sickness is all around you,*
> *journey west for the valley on high.*
> *There you must look for an entrance*

on a path that is hidden from sight.

Search for a sign so familiar
and enter the door in the light.
It will take you on a journey of danger
by steps that are dark but give hope.

Seek a mountain of yellow and purple
through creatures terrible to see.
Harvest the goodness that grows there
to save those at home who may die.

Yet only one on two legs can help you,
and only one who carries our sign.
Guide him, for he will be cub like,
in need of your speed and your fangs.

For the sake of the packs protect him,
give him time to learn and understand
that within him is the power to aid you,
in this dark and most dangerous of times.'

Boy moved around restlessly. What did this all mean?

"I have felt the presence of a child, indeed sensed the Chosen One, a stranger to these lands, growing in my mind. We believe it is the time of the Prophesy."

Boy listened with disbelief. Did they mean him? It couldn't be. He swallowed hard as the Wolf continued.

"The Council fear this sickening amongst us is linked to the soldiers and is the work of the Emperor. We fear he intends to invade and by poisoning us, will remove the protection from our lands. If we are too few, he will invade and overrun us all."

Centra spoke up. "Your news is grievous indeed. How can we help? Are there medicines, or indeed may Wolfrea our Seer offer aid? Do you need warriors?"

Wolvzzar continued. "It may come to war and then yes, warriors from all the villages will be needed. But if we can cure our kin, then we believe the Emperor will not try to overcome us. He would not dare."

"We must cure our kin. We must seek the high valley of the west and there the mountain of yellow and purple. But first, we seek the man cub, the Chosen One. We had thought it would be a child of the villagers but it is my belief that your stranger is indeed the one."

Before he could stop himself, Boy blurted out,

"But I don't know anything. Honestly, I am just a boy, an ordinary boy." He looked around for Luntra and Centra to support him.

Centra smiled. "And yet you carry the mark of the wolf, can speak with the wolf and can walk through solid wooden walls. I do not think many of our children have such skills."

"My child," said Wolvzzar. "We need you to journey with us. We do not know what or why, only that it is told and so must be. We will protect you and bring you back, so you may return to your own lands."

"But he can't go alone, he doesn't know our country or anything about us. He needs someone to teach him." It was

Detra. His voice tailed off as he said, "Mellana and I could teach him."

"Detra is impatient for adventure I think", said Centra. "But he is right. Two warriors will accompany him." He started to cast about to select the right ones when Wolvzzar interrupted.

"Centra, even your fleetest warriors will not match the speed or stamina of the pack and they are too big to carry. Perhaps it is the time of man cubs. Perhaps the two who tried to protect him against us should be chosen. They would be light enough to travel on our backs."

There was a gasp, including Boy. It was crazy for him to journey off to wherever. To ride on a giant wolf would be madness. Before he could say or think anything, there were a host of voices; Detra and Mellana were pleading to go, their parents and other villagers were voicing concerns, Wolfrea was trying to shout above them.

"Silence!", roared Centra, "this is no ordinary time. Our village, our children and children's children are in danger. To fight this evil, we must come together with our friends from the North.

"There is much I do not understand. I am not comfortable that so much burden should be placed on the shoulders of these children. But I believe the coming together of the pack and the stranger is an omen. The Prophesy has been spoken. I believe its time is here. Let the three children go with the pack and find the cure. Who will say 'no' to this, my word?"

A stillness fell over the villagers. The only noise was the rustle of the wind. Boy wanted to scream, *'No this is wrong.*

I am a schoolboy. I am 11 years old. This can't be happening.' But he also remembered Gramdi and her words. 'Take courage. Be strong and you will be safe.' He knew he had to go with the pack. He hugged his knees to his chest, sick with fear.

Wolvzzar spoke gently and Wolfrea, sensing what was to be said, kept her silence but looked across at Boy, smiling in reassurance.

"*I sense your fear my son. Have courage, we will protect you.*" Boy lifted his head, nodded and half-smiled at the wolf, but he couldn't talk.

Then suddenly his back was being slapped. Detra and Mellana were sitting beside him, each grabbing an arm, grinning broadly, both talking at once about what an adventure it was going to be and what an honour to ride a wolf and who would fall off first and he was laughing and yes, he thought, '*a ride on a wolf, a giant wolf. He was going to ride a wolf!*'

Chapter 6 - The Pack Runs

That same day, far away in the mountains of the North, the General shifted the weight of his armour on his shoulders. He looked down on the forest and in the far distance, the plains beyond that led to the South.

"So, this is the land of the wolves. You have done well Colonel. The wolves weaken daily you say. Excellent. Our Lord the Emperor will be pleased. What of the wolves that gathered and then left the forest ten nights ago?"

"I sent men, our best men after them that same day. We do not know their purpose, but I am sure they would not have left the weakened packs unless it was important for their protection. The men have orders to track and kill them and any others they think may threaten us."

The General nodded and smiled grimly. "Soon we will overrun them and then the villages and finally, this land will be ours."

* * *

Boy could not believe that barely two hours later he was standing by Wolvzzar ready to leave. Food and essential equipment prepared and bagged in two baskets for the wolves to carry. Directions given to the mountains of the West. All the villagers had gathered. Detra and Mellana's parents were talking to them earnestly, their faces full of worry. Others were pointing him out and whispering. He hated being looked at. The wolves stood tall and proud, fur glistening in the sun light.

Wolvzzar turned to Wolfrea who spoke his words.

"It is time to leave. It is a right that Longtail bear the weight of Detra. Growler for Mellana and Byter will take you Boy."

A large wolf stepped forward and stood before him. It leaned towards him and sniffed his face. He felt the wolf say, "*You smell strangely Boy.*"

Before he could think of an answer, Mellana ran over to him.

"Detra's telling all the boys what an adventure it's going to be. It is exciting Boy, isn't it?"

Boy didn't know what to say. He couldn't tell her he was frightened, had never ridden before and wanted to be home with Gramdi. He shrugged his shoulders and looked up at Byter.

"I suppose so but, it's a long way down isn't it?"

"It is, but we'll be going very slowly at first, so we can get used to riding." She couldn't help showing her excitement. "And it will be such an honour. Never in the history of our village or any other village has anyone been carried by a wolf." Her parents were calling her to them. "It will be fine Boy, honest."

As she ran off Wolvzzar addressed all the villagers through Wolfrea again.

"We do not know how long the journey will take, only that we will care for your cubs as though they were our own."

So saying he told the three wolves to prepare themselves for the children. Byter lay down beside Boy.

"*Climb onto my back. Try not to be too clumsy.*" Even lying down, Byter was still tall and came up to above his waist. He didn't know what to do. There were so many people watching him. He was also worried about hurting the wolf! Suddenly there were a pair of hands under his arms. He turned to see a smiling Luntra, who easily lifted him up and gently placed him on the wolf's back.

"You can practice getting on when there are fewer eyes upon you." He whispered and laughed as he ruffled Boy's hair.

"Thank you."

Before he could say more he felt the wolf stir beneath him. Boy grabbed Byter's fur to hang on as the wolf slowly got up and suddenly he was looking down a long way at Luntra and the rest of the villagers and the ground.
Centra spoke.

"May the fortunes of this village and land ride with you."
Wolvzzar replied, "And rest upon you."

Boy looked around. Wolvzzar was in front of him. Detra and Mellana were beside him, grinning. Boy just clung on. He was only too aware of how far the ground was below him. He decided he was right, riding a wolf was not going to be fun. Just scary.

The other wolves stood, waiting and watching Wolvzzar, impatient to begin.

"*Ouch. That hurts*", whispered Byter in his mind. "*Try and stay on by holding onto me with your legs rather than ripping the fur out of my coat.*" Boy realised how tightly he was gripping his fur.

"*Sorry Byter.*"

Then Wolvzzar was moving forward and all the pack with him. Byter moved and Boy instinctively gripped his fur again to stop himself falling off.

"*Sorry Byter,*" he repeated as he felt rather than heard the gentle growl beneath him.

As they left the village behind them he became aware how luxuriant the wolf's fur was, beneath his hands. He wanted to stroke it and run his hands through it, but somehow knew that would be wrong.

"*Boy.*" Wolvzzar summoned his attention. "*Boy, the other children cannot hear me. You must speak to them for me. Tell them we will walk for the first hour so you may get used to riding on our backs. Then we must run.*"

Boy shouted across to others and they nodded, like concentrating on staying up. Boy began to take in the countryside. They were heading across gently rolling grasslands, broken up by small woods. To their left the hills where his tunnel lay. In front of them in the far distance, the blue jagged mountains of the West. They looked so far away.

"*Wolvzzar. How long before we get to the mountains where the purple mountain is?*" asked Boy.

"*We do not know. None have travelled that far. Perhaps a moon will rise and fall before we reach there. Come it is time to learn to stay on when we run, hold on. And with your legs remember.*"

Boy warned the others and then felt Byter begin to move more quickly. The ground beneath him was rushing past. Far too quickly. It would be a hard fall if he came off. He felt himself bouncing on Byter's back and tried to hang on, but he was sliding. He shouted out and before he knew it, he felt the wind knocked out of him, his whole body jarring as he thumped into the grass and rolled over and over and over.

Boy groaned and lay still, sure he had broken his back, head and legs. He felt warm breath against his face.

"*Are you hurt?*" Byter was nudging him gently, checking him for injuries. "*You must concentrate. We must hurry.*" The wolf continued to check him over.

"*But I'm hurt,*" Boy moaned.

Byter laughed. "*You will survive. Remember the sick ones we have left at home. Quickly now. Climb on again.*" Boy got up, embarrassed that everyone one was watching him. Byter lay down beside him and Boy scrambled up. He felt Byter growl deep within his chest, as he dug his feet into the wolf's flanks. At last on top, he lay flat along his back, arms around Byter's neck, felt the rich fur against his face and the warmth of his body against him. He concentrated, trying to grip with his thighs and arms, but it was hard and time and again, Byter had to remind him to not to pull on his fur.

As the pace quickened Boy's head started to thump against Byter, so he was forced to hold his head against his neck. He turned to see Detra and Mellana sitting up, concentrating but almost part of their wolves. He tried to sit up a bit, felt his grip go and grabbed a handful of fur. Byter immediately complained. So, he continued to lie against his back as much as he could.

They rode for what seemed like a very long while. His thighs started to ache from gripping. His neck and arms ached. He was relieved when Wolvzzar called a halt.

"*Children you need to give your riders a rest from your weight.*"

Byter lay down for Boy to slide off. The wolf stood up and stretched his back. Boy did the same and was about to sit down and rest properly when Wolvzzar spoke.

"*Boy you must run for a while; my people cannot carry you the whole time.*"

Boy started to panic as he told the others. Detra and Mellana just nodded happily, which made it worse.

Before he could think of any reason not to, or ask why another wolf could not carry him, the pack began to set off. Although their pace was slow, it was faster than Boy was used to running.

He could feel a stitch building up as he struggled to stay with the other two.

"*Wolvzzar, I can't do this,*" he gasped.

The pack stopped and Boy bent over gasping for breath.

"What's the matter?" asked Mellana. "*Are you ill?*" Wolvzzar towered over him, a worried expression on his face.

"*We must push on Boy,*" he said.

Again, the embarrassment. He was beginning to hate this whole thing. He was hot and tired and he ached. He knew he would have to admit he couldn't run fast, never had, never would.

Boy spoke out loud, "I can't run. I'm no good at it. Never have been."

"How can you be no good at it? Everyone runs in our village," said Detra.

Boy felt the blood rushing to his face. "I just can't," he said ashamed.

"*Then we must help you run.*" Wolvzzar interrupted. "*Each of you look for a thick fallen branch, four heads long. I will explain when such a branch has been found.*"

The wolves scattered but soon returned with an assortment of dead branches. Wolvzzar inspected them. Some were too brittle or too thick or too short. He picked up one in his mouth and brought it to Boy. It looked quite like bamboo. Long and thin, but strong.

"*Grapors, you and Fleetfoot hold the branch between you. Boy, stand between them and hold onto it with both hands. We will pull you. We must teach you to run, for there can be no delays.*"

At Wolvzzar's signal, the two wolves held the makeshift pole in their mouths. They lowered their heads so Boy could stand between them, gripping the pole in the middle. Slowly they set off again. He was instantly jerked forward, he thought his arms would come out of his sockets. He stumbled as he was pulled along and felt the pole slipping from his grip. He tripped and fell on his face, the wind knocked out of him. Boy wanted to cry, but knew he couldn't, not in front of the others. He swallowed hard and got up, he tried to ignore the aches and pains that seemed to be all over his body.

Suddenly Mellana was beside him.

"That must have hurt. Look, why don't you bend your arms a bit and hold the branch like this."
He felt himself calming down, pleased she seemed understand. It also meant he didn't have to look at the others.

At first, he struggled to keep up and not be jerked along, but gradually he got into a rhythm. Although it made his arms and shoulders ache, it took much less effort to run. After half an hour Boy was exhausted and gratefully returned to Byter's back, his shoulders, hands and legs burning. But that too was hard work and his legs quickly began to feel numb. Running, riding, running, riding the day seemed to go on for ever.

As the sun set, Wolvzzar declared they would halt in a small copse, by a stream. He heard Detra and Mellana talking about a fire and food and what fun it was and how hungry they were. He ignored them and went to look for the baskets. Two of the wolves had been carrying the baskets in their mouths and had put them down together by a tree. They held essentials for the children and a third, now folded up, to carry the 'goodness' back. He pulled out a blanket. Tired beyond thirst or hunger, he spread it out, lay down on it and glorying in the softness of the grass, fell instantly to sleep.

He was woken by Mellana nudging him, telling him food was ready. He curled back into the blanket and closed his eyes.

"Wake up sleepy head. Time for breakfast." He reluctantly sat up. There were bits of twig sticking into him. He was on the ground. It was half-light.

"Hurry up, Wolvzzar is up and pacing. I think he wants to go."

He opened his eyes. He fought to focus on what was happening. It began to come back to him. What had happened the day before and where he was. It was Mellana and she was holding a leaf out with food of some sort on it. Detra was sitting cross legged nearby eating something similar. The wolves were milling around the edge of the copse.

Boy took the leaf. It looked like brown rice and cooked vegetables of some sort. He was too tired to really notice. He followed Detra's lead and using his fingers tried some. It was delicious. Sweet and soft and savoury all at the same time. He started to wake up properly and realised how hungry he was. All too soon he had finished it.

Detra grinned. "I've never seen anyone sleep as much as you did."

Mellana smiled, "I'm sure it was the right thing to do. It will be easier today."

Boy felt pleased and relieved that they were friendly and not teasing him for being so tired or needing help to run.

"I hope so." He started to stretch. "But everything really aches. I don't understand why other wolves couldn't have carried us?"

Before either of them could answer, Wolvzzar's voice came into his head.

"*Boy we must hurry. Get a drink at the stream and then we must continue.*"

He walked stiffly to the stream, drank thirstily and threw some water over his face. He didn't have time to wash properly and anyway he wasn't sure how. He hadn't brought soap or towels. He stood up, stretched and turned around to find Byter behind him looking down, with deep black and yellow eyes.

"*Time to run Boy but I say this, I wish you were a little lighter.*" Just as Boy felt the colour going to his face, Byter growled a laugh and touched Boys forehead with his nose. "*Come, you look ready to be riding not running for a while.*"

"*Thank you Byter, I am stiff. Will we be running all day? Even longer than yesterday?*" He knew the answer really.

"*Of course, and this time we must try and go a little quicker.*"

Worried and tired in equal parts Boy scrambled up and clung on as the pack began their chase across the plains. The mountains were still just a blue haze in the distance in front of him.

As ever Wolvzzar led. Now they were going faster they fell into line, one behind the other. Wolvzzar and the lead hunting wolves. Then Boy, Mellana and Detra, lastly Longtail and Smorlears carrying the baskets in their mouths.

Boy gradually got used to the increased pace and to his limbs continually aching. Riding, running, riding; the day felt interminable. There had been only the shortest stop for a snatched mouthful of food and then on again. That evening he stayed awake just long enough to eat some food, before crawling into his blanket to instantly fall asleep.

By the end of the third day Boy was still exhausted, aching perhaps even worse, but he was sitting more comfortably on Byter and he was running further and faster than he ever had. He still didn't find it as easy as Mellana and Detra, who seemed to love riding the wolves. He had also gained an appetite and looked forward to their meal together. The food was so tasty, even though he had no idea what it was made from. All the vegetables and fruits looked different and tasted so good!

As he sat eating his meal with Mellana and Detra, Boy turned to Byter and asked why the other wolves didn't share the burden of the children.

"It is because we are descended from those that carried the first stranger to our lands. It was during the Wars of the Ravages. All three died carrying and then protecting her. So, in memory of their sacrifice, only direct descendants from the three may carry a stranger. And that is the reason that only Growler, Longtail and I may carry you. Please, do not ask more, for it is only right that when the tale is told, it is in full. It would not be fitting to rush the telling on this journey. Perhaps when it is all over, there will be such a time."

Boy was full of questions about who the first stranger was and the wars, but he did not want to offend Byter and instead concentrated on his food for a while. The meal over and Boy was thinking about how nice it would be to curl up in his blanket when Detra leaned forward to look at his scar. It was healing, the redness had nearly gone but not the outline.

"Does it hurt?" asked Detra fascinated. Boy shook his head.

"It does look like a wolf you know," commented Mellana.

"Are you sure?" Boy twisted his shoulder to examine it.

"Yes, you can see the outline of the face," Mellana replied as she traced it with her finger.
"His eyes and nose and mouth, here, here and here. It's definitely a wolf." She stared at her finger. "Does it feel warm to you Boy, because my finger is tingling? Can I put my hand against it to check?'

"Sure", Boy replied. "I can't feel anything."
She put her palm against the scar and turned to Detra.

"It is strange. I can feel a heat and tingling going all the way along my arm." She jolted back puzzled. "Didn't you feel anything at all Boy? Nothing?" He shrugged his shoulders and looked at both of them.

"No nothing."

"You do it Detra. Go on," and taking his hand, she placed it against Boy's arm. Boy smiled indulgently at Detra, who half-smiled back. Then his expression turned to alarm and he quickly pulled away and sat away from Boy.

"Mellana's right. I felt the heat go right up my arm. What did you do?"

Boy didn't know what to say. The three of them stared at each other.

"I didn't do anything." He put his own hand against his arm. "See. Nothing. I didn't do anything. Honestly."
The three of them looked at each other. Wolvzzar sensed something was wrong and moved towards them.

"You all look puzzled. Is there a problem?"

"There is," said Detra. "It's Boys arm. The scar, it gives off a heat."

"That's right" agreed Mellana. She gasped and put her hand to her mouth. "I, I understood you Wolvzzar. I understood what you said without Boy saying anything."

"I did too." said Detra. "How can that be?" They both stared at Boy with their mouths open.

Wolvzzar went to inspect and sniff the scar. He placed his nose against it and then nodded. He looked deeply into Boy's eyes. Boy started to wriggle uncomfortably under his gaze.

"There is much to you Boy that none of us understand. I think you may have the powers that the one who came before you had. When you discover them, use them wisely, for all our sakes."

The other two continued just staring at him. Boy felt the colour rise in his face. Things were happening that he didn't understand and that scared him. He was scared because it could mean he was supposed to solve their problems. He was 11 years old. Not 31. It wasn't fair.

"But I don't have any powers. Please what powers? What am I supposed to do?"
Wolvzzar gently touched his face with his own.

"Calm. Be calm. All will be revealed when it should be. We are here to help, guide and protect you. Now," he said, looking all three of them in turn, "it is time for rest. Your riding and running skills have all improved. Tomorrow is a big day, for the pack will run full pace. Come children to bed."

They all stood and looked at each other. Nerves and disquiet were quickly replaced with excitement. Even Boy felt excited at the thought of sitting on Byter when he was running full pace.

"This is going to be great but," Detra pointed to Boy's arm. "What you did with that scar is still weird."

"Ignore him Boy. Wolvzzar's right. It will get sorted. I'm sure of it," Mellana smiled and handed out the blankets.

Later as he lay in bed, waiting for sleep to take him, Boy thought again about his arm, the powers and wondered once more what it all meant.

Chapter 7 - The Pack is Split

That same night, many leagues away a troop of soldiers were wearily resting.

"Captain. We cannot keep up with the pack. Their tracks are becoming older. The horses cannot be ridden longer or faster. They will not survive if we ask more of them."

The Captain took off his helmet. He had not realised how warm this land was. He looked at the troop. All top men. All weary.

"Sergeant. Tell the men to take off their armour. See those trees. Hide the armour and shields. Empty the saddle bags of as much as possible. From now on, we live off the land. We must and will catch them. They would not be making such a journey and at such speed if the survival of the pack did not depend upon it."

* * *

'Shall I get the water Mellana?" asked Boy as he stretched his arms above his head. They had just stopped for the evening. It had been a good day. Day six and the aches and pains were beginning to get less. He had noticed that the countryside was changing, the land was beginning to climb. The trees were less dense but there were still areas of woodland. Grass was giving way to rocky outcrops and moor grass. It reminded him of the moors around Gramdi's house.

Boy went to get the fold-up bucket, made of some sort of leaves sown together, when he tripped on a rock and landed in a small bush. He was cross with himself and then even crosser when he heard Detra laughing at him. He started to get up when he noticed his right foot. The trainer must have caught on the rock because it was ripped on one side.

"Oh no!" he exclaimed crossly and sat down again.

"Are you okay?" asked Mellana. "Have you hurt your foot?"

"It's my trainer. It's ruined. What are Mum and Dad going to say." He groaned. "Mellana, how am I going to carry on without any shoes?" He pointed at hers. They were more like leaves that seemed to curl around her feet. "I haven't got any of those."

Mellana laughed. "Don't worry, I have some spare foot protectors."

"But not my size!" he interrupted. "Unless Detra has the same foot size as me."

"Listen and stop worrying Boy. I don't understand everything you have said, but our foot protectors are for any person. Just stay there."

And before Boy could say anything she went to her basket and pulled out a bundle of thin leaves. They were bigger than his feet, but as thin as a leaf. She peeled two away and put the others back.

"Take off your foot protectors and the thin foot covers and put your feet in the middle of each leaf." She placed two leaves in front of him. He looked at them and then her feet and then Mellana.

"But your shoes are nothing like those leaves."
Mellana and Detra both laughed. "Just put your feet on the leaves and stand still."

Boy shrugged his shoulders and stepped on them. They didn't break as he expected. He was about to move when something strange start to happen. He felt the leaves swelling and growing, like a cushion, under his feet. The ends started to curl around his toes and feet and intertwined across the top of his foot. It felt soft and spongy and a bit tickly as they curled around his toes. He wanted to jerk away, but felt Mellana grab his arm and hold him still. The leaves finally stopped growing. They felt, just perfect. He stepped forward. They were cushioned, so light. Much better than his trainers.

"But how?" He asked them both. They shrugged. "They are picked from a special type of bush. Dad can explain what happens when you put them on, but I get confused. They just are," said Detra shrugging his shoulders.

"Whilst we are on the subject," Mellana bent down into the basket again and pulled out a leafy top and leggings. "Your clothing needs replacing doesn't it?" Boy looked down. He grimaced to himself. He had to admit, his clothing was getting pretty shabby.

"They will fit you. They stretch tight." Boy took them from Mellana. The leaf clothing felt so light and subtle. He went behind the nearest tree and changed. He couldn't believe how comfortable they were.

"I'll get that water now and thanks for the clothes and shoes," he said to Mellana.

"I'll come with you," said Detra. "It'll be good to explore the woods. They look different don't they."

"Be careful both," said Byter, who had left the resting wolves lying down a few metres away. He sniffed the air.

"There are smells here I do not recognise. There is something out there that rules this forest. I do not think it is near, but be careful and stay together at all times. Or shall I come with you?"

"We will be fine Byter. Come on, hurry up Boy." Detra looked back, "I want my tea." Just then Boy ran past him and into the bushes laughing with pleasure and excitement. His new shoes were brilliant. He heard Detra crashing through the undergrowth behind him. Soon, the land dipped and he saw the stream below.

Detra shouted. "Wait a second, let me check it is safe. You do not know the signs. There is something odd here. I can feel it."

Boy looked around him as he ran and ignoring Detra, he rushed on and ran on down the slope, before breaking out into a clearing. It felt strange. Then he stopped. Something felt familiar. He shrugged his shoulders and carried on towards it.

Detra, came out of the wood and shouted out to him.

"Wait. Boy, stop!"

Boy turned around grinned and carried on to the water's edge. Then he heard it. A rustle. In the bushes across the stream. He froze, his blood turning to ice. His heart raced.

A growl. A deep growl. Deeper and more terrifying than anything he had heard in his life. In the undergrowth on the other side of the stream. There was something there.

He gasped. There were two large eyes, blood red in colour, looking at him from the foliage. Then a head appeared. Black as coal. A snarling face, a huge mouth full of fangs and teeth. He felt frozen to the spot. He wanted to turn and run, but his legs wouldn't, couldn't move. All he could do was watch the creature move towards him.

He felt Detra pull him back and step forward to stand in front of him, knife in hand. Staring at the animal, watching its every move, Detra turned to push Boy back towards the trees, his foot slipped and before Boy could react, Detra had fallen onto his back. He cried out in pain, dropped his knife and grabbed his shoulder. Boy looked back up to see a large reptilian creature creep out of the undergrowth, eyes focused on them both.

It was huge. Its body covered in dark scaly skin. Its jaws, full of sharp curved teeth, dripping saliva. One large clawed foot, after another, it slowly stepped towards them, stalking them. Boy was frozen to the spot. He couldn't shout, he couldn't do anything. He heard Detra whimper in pain as he tried to push himself backward against Boy. It reached the water. It bared its large yellow fangs. It crouched as it prepared to jump.

Boy stood there motionless, then suddenly felt a calmness move through him. He stared at the creature. '*No!*' his brain shouted. The animal stopped mid stride and snarled. Unsure of itself. Boy moved forward, stepping over Detra. He raised an arm.

"Go back," he shouted out loud. "Go!"

For a second, a long second, nothing happened. The animal snarled, then it roared defiance, ears pulled back, baring its teeth.

Everything became still. Totally still. No bird or animal noise. Just the animal, Detra, himself. Time itself seemed to stand still. Boy felt the strain of concentrating so hard. He felt a dribble of sweat run down the side of his face. Still he concentrated. He knew that if he relaxed for a second the beast would be upon them. The animal stirred. It backed up a couple of paces, roaring. It was giving in Boy realised. It suddenly turned and ran back into the undergrowth. He felt a wave of relief flood through him. He stood there, staring at the spot where the creature had disappeared back into the undergrowth.

At that moment, Wolvzzar, Byter and Hunnta rushed into the opening and surrounded the boys, sniffing the air and baring their teeth.

"What happened," demanded Wolvzzar. "What was that creature?"

Byter looked down at Detra. "Are you hurt?" Boy came to and dropped down beside Detra, who was gripping his shoulder and rocking backwards and forwards with the pain.

"It's my shoulder. I landed on that rock. I think I have broken something."

"Make way," ordered Wolvzzar. He looked at Boy and then Detra. "Running into the bush. This was badly done Boy, we will speak of it later. Detra, stay very still so I may feel for the damage."

Detra sat up and although his ragged breathing spoke of his pain, he stayed still as Wolvzzar touched his shoulder, front and back, with his nose and face. He stood back and breathed on the area. Detra sighed, the pain vanished from his face though he still looked pale.

Byter came and nuzzled him. "Climb onto my back. I will carry you back to the camp."

Slowly he stood and Boy, feeling wretched helped him as best he could onto Byter's back. Byter trod as carefully as he could to save jolting Detra. Boy followed behind, his head low, he did not want to look at anyone.

At the camp, the others crowded round as Detra slid off Byter's back and lay there, exhausted.

"Can you heal it Wolvzzar. I want to stay with you?" Detra whispered.

Wolvzzar looked down at him. "I cannot mend this hurt, it will need your healer to do that. I have taken away the pain though. It grieves me to say this, but you will need to return to your village and quickly. Longtail will carry you." He turned to the wolf beside him. "Carry him quickly. Rest only when you must. Go then to the Clan, for it will be too late to return to us."

Boy just wished he was home. He quietly edged away from Detra and Wolvzzar and away from the pack. He knew how stupid he had been. *If only I had listened,* he said to himself time and again. But as he sat away from them all, he also remembered the moment of power. It was almost like a heat running through him. He wanted to talk to

Wolvzzar about it, but the thought of facing him made his stomach churn.

He looked across and saw Mellana helping Detra onto Longtail's back. He walked up to them.

"I am sorry Detra, I should have listened to you." Detra half-smiled, "Well you did save my life didn't you. I don't know how you made it go away. But it was very brave of you." Then Longtail was moving and the pack parted to let them him through.

"Run long, run safe. Run for the pack," said Wolvzzar to the departing figures.

Mellana turned to Boy. "What did he mean about you saving his life. I thought Wolvzzar and the others frightened the creature away?"

Boy was too mixed up inside to explain. He felt sick with worry and humiliation. This was all his fault. His fault, that Detra had been hurt and was now having to return to his village. What was Wolvzzar going to say to him? He wanted to tell Mellana what had happened, but he knew it would sound crazy to talk about the power he felt.

"Oh, nothing really. When, Detra slipped, I didn't move, too scared and then Wolvzzar was there." Wolvzzar turned and held Boy with his stare. His eyes bored into him.

"Come it is time. Walk with me Boy." He turned and Boy followed full of dread. They walked to the edge of the grove, where no one could hear.

Wolvzzar turned to him. "Now, tell me what really happened."

Boy felt relieved. Wolvzzar's voice was gentle, he wasn't being shouted at. It gave him the courage to explain as best he could, not only what happened, but about how he felt the power surge through him and the control he felt when he stared down the creature.

Wolvzzar nodded when he had finished and leaned down so that Boy could feel his warm breath upon his face.

"Boy, this is not easy for you. Already you are being asked to leave childhood behind you. This is a time of darkness. I would rather we did not have to ask you to venture into danger, but now is your time. You have a gift, a power, but with that power comes other things. Those around you, look at them Boy."

He looked at the pack as they lay down, ready for sleep, Mellana, busying herself as she put her cooking things away.

"For you to fulfil your destiny and our Prophesy, we will need all our skills and cunning. We are here to protect you, but you in turn must think of others and protect them. And you will best help them by following their advice. This is their land and they know and sense the dangers around us all. Listen to them always, for I sense danger ahead. Do you promise that Boy?"

Boy had been looking at the ground, but looked up and saw not anger but understanding in the wolf's eyes. He half-smiled and nodded gravely and Wolvzzar saw that he had understood.

"Come Boy, let us not forget, you have also shown great courage in facing that animal. That was well done.

Now, it is time you slept. I sense the next days will test us all."

Chapter 8 - A Time for Running

Four days later.

"Fool, what do you mean a wolf and boy slipped past. Why aren't you telling me you caught and killed them both!"

The Captain glared at the soldier. "The boy seems injured you say and returning to the village. Well that is something. Good. Let us hope for your sake the wolf does NOT return." He stabbed the soldier in the chest with his finger. "You would pay dearly for this error if I could afford to lose a man. But do not think it is forgotten. Now get out of my sight."

The soldier hung his head. Bowed and left. He knew answering would gain him nothing. He would have to make amends. He smiled to himself, perhaps he could be the one to kill any remaining children. He hoped it would be so.

* * *

The countryside was continuing to change. The grass was less lush, longer and thinner. The hills steeper and bigger. In the distance, the mountains that had been just a blue haze were beginning to take shape. Jagged snow topped peaks could be seen, cold and threatening.

Boy continued to marvel at the wolves' stamina. They could run for hour after hour. Even the periods Byter and Growler were able to carry them were longer. His legs did not ache so badly from gripping Byter's sides and he now had the confidence to sit upright, moving in tune with the wolf's loping strides. He loved how quiet they were as they moved. The only sound was the wind in his hair as they sped along.

He had stopped needing to hold onto the bamboo pole so much, running rather than being pulled along, during those times when Byter needed to rest his back from Boy's weight. Running was easier in his leaf shoes and leaf clothing. All of it felt as though he was wearing a second skin. Wolvzzar's voice interrupted his thoughts.

"I have been thinking. You need to learn to protect yourself Boy. Mellana.ˮ

"Yes, Wolvzzar."

"I want you to teach him the skills of self-defence. He is to learn the art of the short staff. Let him carry the spare one you have."

Boy was puzzled because it was only just over a metre long and he wasn't sure what use it would be to him or him to it. But he quickly agreed.

It was later that day, when the run was finished that Mellana took out the two staffs. She put one down and held the other in front of him.

"Take it'," she said. He gasped at the weight of it. "It is wood from a tree that grows in the forests towards the North. Now watch."

She took the staff back, turned around and gripping one end in both hands, swung it as hard as she could. It smashed through a tree branch next to her, as though the branch was made of glass. Boy looked at the branch, now on the ground and marvelled at how clean the cut had been. He realised it was as deadly as any sword.

"Boys and girls are taught the art of the staff from five years old. You will only have time to learn the basics, so every day, I will teach you how to protect yourself with it against any animals that may attack you." From her pack she pulled out what he realised was a long line of twine. Except it wasn't twine he realised when he felt it, but thin tree bark.

"We will tie up the ends so you can wear it across your back at all times. Let's start with holding the staff."

And so, every night and morning, Boy would spend time learning how to hold the staff, how to stand and defend himself with it. Mellana was a patient teacher and he was amazed how quickly he began to follow the moves she taught him. Although he was always tired at night after a day's travel, he enjoyed learning how to use the staff as though it was an extension of his arm.

Several days later they came to the river. They had crossed minor ones many times. Mostly they had been narrow and shallow. Occasionally, a faster running one, wider and deeper. Deep enough to have been a problem for Mellana and he, but the wolves had been able to walk across with the two of them barely getting their feet wet.

This one was different. Steep banks either side meant they were looking down on the river several metres below. It was several hundred metres across with deep channels of fast flowing current. Like the fingers on a giant hand, these channels were separated by sections of exposed river bed, where gnarled bushes grew out of smooth grey stones.

"Byter, Growler," said Wolvzzar. "Mark the opposite bank further down the river. See how the bank drops? We shall aim to cross and land there. Boy and Mellana, you shall ride on their backs. The water is too deep and swift for you to cross alone. Come."

Boy had never been a good swimmer. He had always hated school swimming lessons. Now he looked at the furthest part of the river, beyond the stones and smaller channels and streams. The speed with which the far channel flowed looked frightening. The dark colour suggested a much deeper water than they had encountered before. He bit his lip and felt his stomach clench at the thought of falling off Byter and being carried downstream.

Mellana reassured him. "Don't worry, we will be fine. Byter will make sure you are safe."

"I know," said Boy. "I just don't like swimming much, especially in cold, fast rivers." He laughed but knew it sounded false.

Byter joined in. "Well Boy. I may decide to keep you from falling off. But I may change my mind and drop you in half way across, if you continue to grip my fur like that." Startled, Boy looked down and saw his knuckles were white from gripping the wolf's back hair. He instantly let go.

"Sorry Byter. I didn't realise."

Byter laughed and then all conversation was forgotten as they slid down the bank on to the stony shore.

The first few channels were shallow and Byter easily walked through them onto the raised stony riverbeds. Mellana in front of him, turned and grinned with reassurance as they reached the stones after a deeper and broader channel. Boy began to gain hope that it would be okay. Perhaps the last big channel would be alright after all.

He soon knew he had been wrong. Closer to, the channel looked deeper and swifter and more dangerous than ever.

"You will need to hang on me during this part Boy. Yes, even gripping my fur if necessary. I may have to swim this last bit. I have never crossed anything this fast moving before."

Wolvzzar stood overlooking the channel, the other wolves gathered around him. Boy could not hear what he was saying, but it was obviously deep and fast even for them. The drop here was sudden and steep. It meant they could not be sure of their footing, once they moved down into the fast-moving water.

The large wolf, Hunnta stepped forward first and slid down. He was immediately swept off his legs by the current, went under the water but he quickly resurfaced. He struggled to gain foot holds and was swept along again. At the third attempt he managed to stand facing the current. The water came up to the top of his legs. By now, he was further downstream, near to the shallow bank where Wolvzzar wanted him to land. With a heave he managed to leap forward and, in several bounds, made the shallower water and then the river bank. Sylvabak was next and Boy again watched with fear and then relief, as he managed to struggle across.

Wolvzzar turned to Boy and Mellana. "We shall go as four in a line. Growler, Byter, Runlong and myself. Boy if you or Mellana fall into the water, Runlong and myself will be there to save you. Fleetfoot and Smorlears, will cross next as you carry the baskets. Grapors shall cross last."

Boy felt his heart pounding as they went to the water's edge. All four wolves stood in a row waiting for Wolvzzar's command. Sylvabak and Hunnta were poised on the other bank to re-enter the water if Boy or Mellana fell in. To Boy the seconds felt like minutes.

"Now," said Byter as a warning. Boy gripped with his legs as hard as he could, as Byter began to slide almost out of control down the stones and into the channel.   He dropped his body down onto Byter's back as he was jerked around. Then they were in the water with a giant splash. The shock of the cold water around his legs and arms and body made him gasp. He felt Byter scrabbling for grip on river bed, felt him lose his balance and fall sideways under the water. He hung on, eyes shut tight as his head went under. He felt the cold river water rushing over his face and then he was choking and coughing and gasping for air as Byter fought his way upright again. He clung on, clothes soaking wet, shivering. It was harder than ever to hold onto Byter's now slippery sides.

They were nearly half way across. Boy shook his head to clear the water from his eyes. Growler was behind them, also struggling to keep his footing in the fast-moving current. He couldn't see Wolvzzar or Runlong. His heart was pounding, too terrified to think straight, all his thoughts on how to stay on. Then he saw, almost in slow motion, Growler begin to slip and fall to the side. He heard Mellana's scream as she fell with him into the water. Growler quickly gained his balance and jerked up onto his feet, but so quickly that Mellana lost her hold and slid back into the river. The wolf turned to grab her, but lost his balance again and went under the water.

Without thinking, Boy sat up straight, saw that Hunnta and Sylvabak were jumping back into the water, but would be too late to save Mellana. He tore the staff off his back and leant forward along Byter's back, pointing it out in front of them.

"Where is she Byter? I can't see her."

Mellana surfaced, the current quickly pulling her towards them. Holding onto the end of the staff with one hand and the back of Byter's neck with the other, Boy screamed above the noise of the water, "Grab the staff Mellana. The staff! Grab it!" and desperately waved it at her.

She was nearing them, her face just clear of the water, frantically swimming to stop herself from being carried further away from them. She saw the staff, made a lunge and caught the end of it. The current took her under again. Boy felt the staff nearly pulled out of his hand and then his arm being jerked hard. He felt himself slipping, grabbed Byter's fur, but the water had made it slippery. He couldn't hold on and was dragged off Byter into the river. He held onto the staff, the freezing water swirling around him. He felt the current pulling him around and down.

Suddenly, he was being hauled back upwards and his head was out of the water. It was Byter, holding him by the back of his tunic, which dug into his armpits. The water roared in his ears. He gasped for breath as Byter lifted him clear. But then Byter lost his footing and the three of them were pulled under the water again. Byter surfaced and the chain of three were hurtling downriver. Water streaming down his face, he saw Mellana, gripping the staff grimly with both hands as one moment she was gasping for breath, the next being pulled under by the current.

Hunnta and Sylvabak were now in position in front of them. Byter released his grip on Boy, as Mellana and then Boy were caught and lifted by their tunics by the two wolves. Mellana let go of the staff and the pain in his arms and hand disappeared, but then the tunic bit harder under his arms as he was lifted higher by Hunnta.

Jumping and lurching sideways, they gradually all stepped towards the shallower and calmer waters. Hunnta held onto Boy as they unsteadily moved through the calmer water to a shallow sandy bank, where they joined the others. He sank to the ground and saw Mellana do the same. Boy was exhausted and his shoulder ached badly but his first thought was for Mellana. He was relieved to see her sitting up, shaken but smiling. He moved and sat down beside her.

"Thank you, Boy. That was frightening wasn't it. I'm sure I would have been swept away if you hadn't helped me." She leaned across to hug him. Boy felt embarrassed and didn't know what to say. But he found himself smiling as he stuttered that it was okay.

They were both soaked again as the wolves shook their fur, showering the children with droplets of water. They spluttered and laughed in surprise and relief.

Byter came up to Boy. "Told you not to worry Boy," he laughed quietly.

One by one the remaining wolves came ashore, Smorlears and Runlong still clutching the now wet baskets for Mellana and Boy.

Wolvzzar stood before them "You did well children. Boy, using your staff. That was clever. It gave time for Hunnta and Sylvabak to get into position. You have learned much."

"Thank you Wolvzzar."

"It was quick thinking Boy," Byter nudged his face. "It was also very brave of you. Well done." Boy grinned. He nudged Byter's head back.

"You saved us both Byter. Thank you for today and for all the other days." For a moment they stayed face against face.

Then Wolvzzar was calling Byter and he sat there, cold but content as Byter loped away. He continued to grin to himself. He couldn't help it. He had never been thought of as brave before. He had never been in so scary a situation and to help save Mellana as well! Yes, today was a very good day.

Chapter 9 - The Prophesy Remembered

Two days after the wolves had crossed the water, the captain turned back in his saddle. The river crossing had been hard, very hard. But they came from a land of rivers and none had been lost. The men looked soaked and bedraggled.

"Troop, Attention! You are supposed to be the best. So, show it!

"It will not be many days now. Then you can have your revenge for being wet and cold. These wolves are not difficult to follow. Clear tracks and the occasional carcass. Yes, soon we will be upon them."

The troops began to sit up straight, but barely acknowledged him, too tired and wet to answer.

* * *

The wolves made steady progress over the coming days. Since the river crossing, the country had risen steeply and it had been hard on them all. But now they were on high lands. As they climbed, the mountains ahead were becoming clearer. Byter thought it would be at least seven more days before they reached them.

His work with Mellana each evening, practicing self-defence with the staff was fun, despite the tiredness he felt. Mellana said that he showed real promise. He had never been good at any sort of sport and yet here he was running and learning combat methods. He knew he had so much more to learn. Mellana could run three or four times as long as he could. And she was so fast with the staff.

"Keep up Boy," whispered Byter, "Wolvzzar wants to gain time on these flatlands. The mountains ahead will test us. Try to be swifter." The stitch kicked in as Byter spoke. He grimaced. Maybe he wasn't that fit after all.

It was ten days later. No trees, no hills, no nothing. Just flatlands of coarse grass and scrub. Ten days of running and riding. Every day the same, except for the mountains, at least they had grown closer and closer. Finally, they had arrived near the cliff base.

Wolvzzar called a halt and they rested briefly. The cliffs towered above them but between them and the rocky heights was a gorge dropping several hundred feet. At the bottom a meandering river. Boy could see the climb down would be difficult and dangerous. There was no clear path and the ground looked loose and slippery. One false step and he could fall all the way to the bottom. That was not the worst of it. If they managed to cross the gorge, they faced cliffs that rose and rose. The mountains looked so steep. Impossible to climb, especially for the wolves.

Mellana shook her head, "They are like the mountains of Chylgar. How are we going to climb up there?"

"And yet we must," said Byter, "for we cannot go around them. Come, Wolvzzar wants us all. He will know what to do."

They joined the other wolves gathering around their leader. No one was speaking, all of them waiting patiently as Wolvzzar, sat staring at the cliffs.

Boy studied the cliffs again. The dark rock looked menacing in the evening light. Behind the cliffs and set back, were the mountains. Not as steep as the cliffs and covered in trees, they seemed to rise forever. Above the tree line, bare rock and snow. Too high to climb. So high they looked as if they might almost be touching the sky. Wolvzzar addressed them all.

' When sickness is all around you,
journey west for a valley on high.
There you must search for an entrance
on a path that is hidden from sight.'

"The Prophesy has been with us for countless generations. It is why we have made this journey. There must be a way. And yet I see no valley, no shallowing of these cliffs. Nor have I these past days as we have drawn nearer."

"Perhaps the entrance is elsewhere. Let me run South and Hunnta run North?" suggested Runlong. Wolvzzar slowly nodded his head.

"We have been watching the cliffs these last four days. Always we have run due West. I am sure there has to be another answer. We stay here for the night. Perhaps the answer will be clearer in the morning light."

Runlong pawed the ground for attention.

"Smorlears and I speak for the South pack. We agreed that the journey had to be made. We agreed that the Prophesy had not been handed down from generation to generation without reason. But we do not know for sure it was for now that the Prophesy spoke. "We have willingly run at your command these many days. But if by tomorrow there is no path ahead, we believe we need to rethink the way forward."

Others agreed with her including Hunnta.

"Wolvzzar, every pack here respects your lead. We all heard your words at the Council of Wolves. But if there is not a way forward here, surely at least, we have to look North and South for an answer?"

"Hunnta, Runlong, I understand why you say this, but we are so short of time," Wolvzzar replied. "The Prophesy speaks of a valley. I do not believe the Prophesy will be proved wrong. There are times when the solution is in sight but not seen. Sometimes the answer has to reach out to us not us rush to seek it."

He looked up and around him. In the same steady tone, he continued.

"The evening is upon us. Let each of us think and watch as we await the dawn." Without another word, Wolvzzar got up and wandered off to sit alone, upright, staring at the cliffs for the elusive valley. The other wolves sat or prowled around, saying little.

Mellana suggested they use the time practicing with the staff, but after several hard knocks, they both realised their hearts weren't in it. Byter came and lay down beside them. As had become their habit in the evening, they both leaned against him, except this time it was for comfort, for they were both unsure of what would happen next.

"Byter," said Boy, "what happened at the Council of Wolves, you know before you started this journey."

"Before the Council, came the sickness," Byter replied. "It came upon us over one moon's rise and fall."

Boy took that to mean a month.

"My brother and sister were out hunting. They had found a weak deer. It was odd for it seemed dazed and made no effort to escape. They killed it and began to eat, but it tasted bitter and so left it. On their return to the pack a dizziness, a weakness and a pain, such pain came upon them. Others in the pack began to fall ill. Soon most of our pack was ill. Then we heard that members of other packs were also afflicted."

"We think it is linked to the soldiers from across the mountains. All this happened soon after they had been sighted near the old tunnels. There has always been the occasional man or animal that has strayed or tried to cross into our lands. Always we have turned them back, for they only seek to conquer and kill." The children listened, enthralled. ·

"But this was different. These were soldiers, soldiers in armour. They tried to attack us with spears. Even after they caught and butchered Longears, who was no more than a pup, Wolvzzar would not have them killed. Many of us wanted revenge but he reminded us that true strength at times lies in restraint. And so, we cornered and disarmed them. Returned them to the tunnels to show them our strength and for them to take back the message that this, our land was not for them. Or so we thought." He paused remembering.

"Yes, it was soon after that the sickness started. We fear it is somehow to do with them and now we are too few to guard the entrance properly. It was there, at the Council that we discovered how the other packs had caught the sickness, they too believed it started with a kill. Several have been lost from each pack and I fear for my brother and sister. If a cure is not found then all the packs will be endangered."

Boy felt Mellana take his hand. He gripped it back in return, sensing the worry and sadness in Byter.

"It was then, at the Council that the Prophesy was recited by Wolvzzar and the cause of much debate. Many were not convinced of the Prophesy. An old tale for telling to young pups some thought."

"But," he sighed, "no other way forward could be suggested or agreed upon. So, two from each of the other packs joined Wolvzzar and I for this journey. It is a desperate decision yet I believe in Wolvzzar. He is strong and wise. He leads us all. I believe seeking the Valley will be first test of the Prophesy. Let us hope tomorrow brings the answer that he seeks from these cliffs."

Mellana and Boy said nothing. They rested against Byter's side, taking comfort from his presence and his warmth. Little was said by anyone that evening. A sadness and tension hung over them all. Later as Boy prepared for sleep, he saw that Wolvzzar had not moved. He remained like a statue, sitting on his haunches, staring at the cliffs, willing them to give up their secret.

When Boy awoke the next morning, Wolvzzar was in the same place. He and Mellana whispered about what they should do. Mellana suggested the two of them should try and climb the cliff, but fortunately she decided it was not practical. They went quiet and stood side by side wondering what would happen. Runlong spoke first.

"Wolvzzar, it is time for us to decide a way forward. We can't stay here and if we cannot go on, do we look to the north and south of this point or return to our packs?" Others joined in with different views, whilst Wolvzzar sat quietly and listened to them.

Boy found himself distracted by the sunlight. It was a cloudy day, but now and again, the clouds separated and the sun shone down, in a sharp narrow beam, only to disappear as the clouds swirled about. It gradually moved along the cliff face, making the outline and features of the cliff as clear as if they were much closer.

The sun went in, only to return a minute later, on the cliff face in front of them. It shone all the way down the cliff face to the ground. It moved again, except this time it seemed to stop a hundred metres or so from the ground. Puzzled Boy kept watching. The beam moved with the clouds. It continued to shine, except it still stopped short of the ground. He gasped, sat up straight and pointed.

The cliff. It wasn't a single cliff face. There was a gap. There had to be a small lower cliff that was somehow proud of the main cliff. Same colour as the main cliff, the small cliff was somehow blending into the main one. It had to be separate from the main cliff. That's why the sun stopped short of the ground. The way up could be hidden behind the small cliff that was proud of the main one.

"Look! Look, the cliff. It's not a cliff."

He couldn't think of the words. Others turned to look at him. He pointed furiously, but the beam of sunlight had gone already. Boy could feel the Wolves' irritation.

"What is it you think you saw?" said Hunnta.

Boy felt his face go red and hot. He looked at Hunnta and then quickly back at the cliff. He didn't want to lose the spot. The sun beams had gone completely, leaving the cliff looking dark and brooding. It had gone. The place had gone.

"The sun, it shone on the cliff, I think the cliff is split there and there is a way up somehow." He stammered. He felt the disbelief as the wolves and Mellana looked at him and then the now sealed cliff face.

"I cannot see anything, can anyone?" demanded Runlong. "Are we to risk the climb down and out of the gorge, because Boy thinks he saw for a second, something that we cannot see?"

Sylvabak stepped forward. "Wolvzzar, the cub proved himself in the river, but do we risk the climb down on what he may have seen? What is your decision?"

Wolvzzar remained silent. He was staring at Boy. He felt the intensity of the stare and had to look away. The wolf stood. He slowly moved up to him.

"Let us hear him properly. Tell me again Boy, what you saw and where?"

"Wolvzzar you are putting off the moment, he saw nothing," complained Smorlears. "None of us can see anything."

"Let him speak. Remember, he is no ordinary cub." The others backed away, deferring to Wolvzzar.

Boy's heart was thumping and his mouth was dry. What if I didn't see anything. What are they going to say? he thought to himself.

"*Courage child.*" A voice deep inside him prompted. It was Wolvzzar and he instinctively knew no one else had heard it. He took a deep breath and explained what he had seen. He still stumbled over describing what he had seen and what he thought it meant, but this time he could see some of the pack believing him.

Wolvzzar turned to the others.

"I like you cannot see the small cliff or gap. But I will not give up on our packs so easily. Come Boy, take the lead with Byter and show us what you have found."

Chapter 10 - The Boy Leads the Way

The Captain could not remember when he ached so badly. He had never spent so long in the saddle. He cursed these upland plains that seemed to go on forever. Too many times a day he was forced to order the troop to run beside the horses, to save them. But he would not give up.

The mountains were close now. Two days behind still, according to the tracker. He had better be right. He stretched again to ease his aching back. He would catch them though. Then he would make them pay for making him take this journey. Yes, they would pay dearly.

* * *

Wolvzzar led the way down into the river gorge. It was steep, but he followed the old tracks that sheep or goats had used in the past. The two children went next. Boy following Mellana with Byter behind. He could not look down. The drop was too great and he didn't much like heights.

He kicked a stone by mistake and watched as it crashed down and down collecting other stones on the way, before finally splashing into the river. The ground on this side was slippery and with too many loose stones. He was sure he would slip. He picked out his way carefully, his hand searching for anything to hold onto. Occasionally he felt Byter steady him by holding the back of his tunic.

Suddenly there was a scrabbling of paws as Grapors lost her footing. He feared seeing her hurtling down the cliff side, but when he carefully looked back they were all still in a line behind Byter. Mellana kept turning around to warn him of loose stones or slippery footings. It seemed to take forever, and he felt exhausted by the time he reached the gorge floor. He let out a great sigh, grinned and thanked both Mellana and Byter.

It was a bonus they realised, that the river was not fast flowing and only knee high for Boy and Mellana so they were able to wade across safely.

The climb back up was less scary, but hard work and Boys legs were aching badly by the time they reached the top. But the aching was nothing compared to the nervousness and self-doubt he was feeling. What if the gap didn't exist? What if it was just an optical illusion? He cringed inside, at the thought of what Hunnta would say. More importantly he would have let Wolvzzar down, again.

They stumbled up on to the flatland and Boy immediately started searching around.

"Can you see it Boy?" asked Mellana urgently.

"No, I can't. I'm sure it was around here though." He felt the wolves watching him as he searched the cliffs from left to right. It had to be here. He was sure of it.

He felt the rising panic. It had to be here. He caught sight of Runlong, pacing backward and forward. He knew he had to find it soon. Perhaps he had made a mistake. Perhaps it had been some sort of trick of the light afterall.

He made himself take a deep breath and walk along scouring the cliffs once more, slowly from left to right.

He stopped. He gasped and then grinned.

"There, look!" Boy cried out and pointed. The cliff wasn't whole. Proud of the main cliff face was a thin hillock. From the front it looked as though it was one cliff. But to the side, yes, it had a gorge separating the small hillock from the cliff. There WAS a gap. Byter stopped with Growler for the children to climb on and together they all ran for the cliff.

The gap was quite small, just three metres across. A small stream had gradually eaten away the rock creating a sloping gorge and a hidden path that lead from the base of the cliff. Wolvzzar turned to Boy.

"You have keen eyes. Yet again you have proved your worth to the pack."

Byter and the others were all full of praise and Boy felt embarrassed, pleased and relieved all at the same time.

"It was a good job you were watching those sun beams Boy," said Mellana as they began up the gorge slope. "I don't think we would have seen it otherwise."

Boy just grinned again and then had to cling on as Byter began the ascent in earnest.

The climb was easier than the river gorge but still required care. Boy noticed that amongst the small rocks, there were bits of slabs, as though there was a staircase there many, many years ago.

As Byter crested the cliff top, Boy gazed around. The ground continued to slope up, but for a few hundred metres was fairly flat. Then the mountain face rose steeply, but now instead of bare rock, it was covered in trees. Boy was amazed how they seemed to cling on despite the angle of the cliffs. The line of trees was broken by two shards of rock about twenty metres tall and several metres wide. Between them no trees grew, instead the rock face was covered by a dark green moss.

Everyone was confident this had to be the way forward, the doorway spoken of in the Prophesy, but how to get through it was a different matter. Wolvzzar took the lead and walked up to it. He sniffed the moss and pawed it.

"This is much clearer. There must be a doorway, behind the moss."

As one, wolves and children began to paw or pull the moss away from the rock face. It came away easily, but only appeared to reveal yet more rock face. They all stood back to search for signs.

"What was the verse again Byter," asked Mellana. The wolf repeated it.

'There you must look for an entrance
on a path that is hidden from sight.
Search for a sign so familiar
and enter the door in the light.
It will take you on a journey of danger
by steps that are dark but give hope.'

Wolvzzar turned to them. "I think we should look for the sign of the wolf." He looked back at the rock wall. "Again, it is a puzzle that time and sharp eyes may have to solve." He looked at the darkening sky. "The day is near to its end. I think we will have to wait till morning." He stopped, looked at the wall and then across the plains,

"Yes, I think it is going to be sensible to await the morning."

They were settling down to sleep when they first heard it. A piercing screech. Everybody jumped up to look for what had made the noise. The wolves immediately formed a ring, facing outward. The children were herded into the middle.

"What was it?" Boy looked around him. "Byter is it dangerous?" He immediately knew it was a silly thing to say, but it was scary and the fact the wolves were reacting so, made him more scared.

"Be still Boy, we need to listen." Wolvzzar's calming voice quietened him.

He looked to Mellana and they grimly smiled at each other. After five minutes, Wolvzzar told them to settle, but posted Grapors and Smorlears with instructions that the camp should be guarded all night.

The second screech shook him awake. He had been in a deep sleep. He felt disorientated, trying to think straight, whilst the wolves moved quickly and silently around him. He could see nothing.

"Where did the noise come from?" he whispered to Mellana. He felt her shrug in the dark,

"I don't know. Seemed as if it was above us."

This time the wolves remained as they were. The screeches continued. Sometimes nearer, sometimes further away, but always from above. Boy slept little. He was exhausted, but every time he started to slip into sleep another cry would wake him.

The screech again, but this time much closer, followed by a beating of wings. It sounded huge, but that made no sense.

"We have no such bird," said Byter and Mellana agreed. Boy looked out across the plains, it was getting light in the East. It would soon be dawn. Then a screech and a shape, it was huge, coming towards them. A wolf standing and leaping sky wards, a howl of pain and giant claws above him. A whoosh of wings and wind on his face and it was gone.

Wolvzzar's voice, "Smorlears, are you badly hurt? No. Good. Come to me all of you. It is a giant bird. Watch for the claws."

Boy followed Byter's instruction for them both to stay near the ground. The seconds and minutes seem to go on for ever. The screech again.

Boy scoured the sky looking for the creatures. The light was improving every second.

"There," he shouted and pointed up, seeing the dark shape, wings outstretched dropping towards them, screeching again and again. The wolves stood proudly, like bait as the claws approached, ducked as it went overheard and jumped up to bite the backs of its legs as it sailed past. Immediately a second one came from another direction, but pulled away when it saw the prepared line of teeth awaiting it. The sky was streaked with yellow and two, no three birds, Boy counted, circled above. Long necked, huge gliding wings and massive viscous claws. He realised with horror, they were so big, they could carry off one of the wolves.

"Back to the doorway. They cannot so easily attack there," ordered Wolvzzar and as one the wolves moved backwards, whilst keeping on watch for another attack. Boy and Mellana knelt against the cliff wall, protected by the wolves in front of them.

The birds circled, but as the sun began to rise, so did the number circling. Three became five then six.

"Pack, they are gathering for an attack. Be ready." Wolvzzar's voice calm despite everything. "The sun will soon be our faces. It will be difficult to see them."
The screeching was continuous. Boy covered the sun with his hands and watched with horror as they began to circle closer and closer. Their heads were strange. Even at a distance, he could see they did not have beaks, but long leathery faces and when they screeched, he could see the rows of teeth.

An attack was bound to happen, and with the number and their claws and teeth, he understood the danger they were in. He saw them turn in towards them. Boy suddenly felt the fear begin to drain away, replaced by an anger. Mellana and the wolves were his friends. He would not let them be hurt.

He glared at the birds as they banked and swooped down towards them. Faster and faster they came, screeching, their claws outstretched. '*Nooooo!*' he screamed in his head. '*Get back!*' his mind shouted above the terrible screeches. Instantly they broke away in confusion. The screeching resumed and became continuous as they circled again. They came a second time and again he screamed at them in his mind to go away. As before they backed off and circled.

"Why do they sheer off?" he heard one of the wolves ask.

"Stay calm and in place. Be grateful they do." Came Wolvzzar's order.

The sun became blinding as it rose completely across the plain. The birds gathered again, circling closer and closer. The noise was deafening. Suddenly there was a loud jarring noise behind them.

"Look," Mellana cried out. "The rock. It's the entrance." Except it wasn't one. It was a gold outline of a huge double door and in the middle was an image. An image of a wolf's head.

"Boy, put your hands on the wolf head." Wolvzzar shouted. "Quickly, before they attack again."

He stood up and placed both hands at the centre of the giant image. He felt his hands growing warm and tingle, felt the rock shiver. The screeching again. He turned his head to see the birds were attacking. He shouted in his mind, but without time to gather himself, they kept coming. Realising what was about to happen, he turned around and screamed at the top his voice.

"Noooooooo!" The wolves jumped at his scream and watched with amazement as the lead bird with his talons outstretched was suddenly blown backwards into two birds behind. Boy watched as they all frantically flapped their wings to veer away, their screeching now one of alarm.

Behind him he could hear a grating sound. He turned, the rock outline had become doors. Rock doors that were opening inwards.

"Quickly inside," roared Wolvzzar and they turned and fled into the doorway. Boy felt his body lifted by his collar as though he weighed nothing. Feet dangling, he was whisked into the cavern. Byter dropped Boy gently to the ground.

"Best to look from in here I thought." he said.

"Thank you Byter," smiled Boy as he reached up to pat his flanks. On all fours he looked up and watched in fascination as the birds, one after another landed on the ground outside the doorway, confused about how to pursue their attack. With all the wolves safely inside and keeping guard, Boy turned to look at the cave.

It had three columns on either side chiselled out of the bare rock. Beyond them and cut into the back wall was a tunnel entrance. The entrance was framed by two stone figures, taller than the wolves. One held an open book whilst the second had been damaged and only the stumps of his arms remained. Inside the entrance was a series of steps that were quickly lost in the tunnel darkness.

He heard Wolvzzar intoning the Prophesy.

'It will take you on a journey of danger,
by steps that are dark but give hope.'

Just as he finished the doors started to groan again. This time they were shutting.

"Hold the doors open. They must not be allowed to shut, we will need to return this way," ordered Wolvzzar and several of the wolves hurled themselves at the doors, their feet slipping on the cold stone floor as the doors continued to close. Byter and Growler joined them. Then the doors were slowing. They groaned and shuddered to a halt, still half open.

Mellana was gazing at the ceiling.

"Look Boy, at those creatures. I have never seen anything like them before."

Some of the carvings were of men, some of a forest, and at the far end, strange creatures. In the middle a carved crown or circlet, with six raised stones in the shape of six men sitting. Strange he thought.

"Well done everyone. Well done." Wolvzzar walked through the group nodding to each of them.

"I do not know where this will lead, but to hope and danger. We must be on our guard. Come, it is time to leave these birds."

Boy was about to comment on the carved creatures above him, when Mellana pulled on his arm and together they followed Byter towards the tunnel entrance and the darkness beyond.

Chapter 11 - The tunnel end

The gorge lay beneath them. The river looked calm enough, but the path, that would be tricky. A noise, a screeching attracted his attention. He looked up. Birds. But such birds. They were giants. His instincts told him they were hunters. Yes, they would need watching.

"Sergeant, we rest until late afternoon. We must risk an evening crossing. I do not trust those creatures above us."

* * *

Mellana caught up with Grapors who was carrying her basket. She thanked her and as they walked along, Mellana reached in and pulled out a tiny cage. She opened the floor of it and took out what looked like a large brown nut. She peeled it to reveal a large slug. It curled and twisted in her hands as she pushed it into the cage and reclosed it. Suddenly the slug changed colour from white to orange and then began glowing. A soft light filled the tunnel showing the way.

Boy could now see the steps were smooth and worn. Obviously very old. He realised that they continued as far as the light carried. And always upwards. He could see the marks on the roof and walls where it had been chiselled out. Neither Byter or Mellana could explain who had done this or who had lived here. The air was stale and the steps built for men not wolves. It was hard work for all of them. After what seemed hours, Wolvzzar called for a break.

Little was said for a few minutes then Mellana spoke.

"Wolvzzar, why couldn't the birds attack. I mean, why did they duck away?" Boy felt the wolf's large eyes looking deeply into him.

"I think Boy can best explain it. We all felt it Boy." Mellana with a look of puzzlement on her face stared at Byter, then turned to Boy. and then back to Byter. Boy looked down. He avoided her gaze, he felt embarrassed again. But no one spoke, they were all waiting for his answer.

"I feel a power," he whispered, almost to himself.

"What do you mean?" said Mellana. "What power and what's that got to do with the birds?"

Boy looked pleadingly at Byter, who nodded encouragingly.

"I seem to be able to understand animals and they me. It was like the animal that wanted to attack Detra and me." He looked at Mellana and was relieved to see she wasn't laughing, she was listening. It gave him confidence.

"I feel this power. I feel it throughout me. When it's in me, I can command animals to stop attacking me. And the power, like an invisible force, just flows from me towards them. It's only happened a few times and I don't really understand it."

He didn't know if he was making any sense. "At home there is a dog. Everybody is afraid of it. But it comes to me and is friendly because I like it." He couldn't think of anything else to say.

Mellana sat there wide eyed. The fact the wolves felt the power, meant it had to be real.

"So, does that mean that you can tell any animal what to do?" she asked.

"I don't know. I can speak to Wolvzzar and the others here, but..." he shrugged his shoulders. "I can only talk to you all, because you can talk to me. I don't understand it really."

"Do you have to say special words or do something with your hands or something?" Mellana was clearly intrigued by what she had heard.

"No, I just feel it when it's gathering inside me."

Wolvzzar spoke. "I believe you have been called here to protect the Land and to use your powers to save it. I do not fully understand but I, indeed all of us, recognise the power that lies within you Boy. It is how you use it and when that will become important. Like any gift, it is to be used wisely."

Boy hoped he would be wise. He didn't really understand everything Wolvzzar said and he felt a bit nervous about the idea of protecting the land from something. It seemed a lot to ask. Then Wolvzzar was rising.

"Come, we are here without food and water and I do not know how far we must travel."

The journey continued. It seemed like it would never end. The walls and ceiling were bare, the steps worn. Whoever lived here must have been very successful to have been able to dig such a tunnel, he thought. His legs were aching. The steps were not large, but they were wide and deep and he had to stretch for each step. He had no idea how long he had been climbing. Then another stop. More walking and climbing. His legs now rubbery, were struggling to keep up. Byter leaned forward.

"Get onto my back Boy, I can see you are exhausted." Boy just shook his head. He had heard Byter slipping on the stones. Knew he must be as hot and thirsty and exhausted as he was.

They carried on. Boy didn't think he could walk much further. He had lost all sense of time. All he could do was focus on lifting his feet and putting them down one in front of each other.

Later, much later, Wolvzzar called a halt.

"We rest here for the night. Sleep as you can." The wolves as one lay down across the steps. Boy curled up alongside them, too tired to worry about how uncomfortable it was.

All too soon, he awoke. He was on his side. He was stiff and sore. The air though was still stale and stuffy. His throat was so dry. He rubbed his eyes. Mellana was there, kneeling in front of him.

"You fell asleep before I could give you this." It was a fruit. Like an apple but brown in colour. "I found it at the bottom of the basket."

It looked battered and bruised, but he hungrily took a lump out of it. It was so good and sweet. He savoured the juices, that squirted into his so dry mouth as he took a second bite.

He looked up and saw the longing in her face. Smiling with his mouth full, he offered her the rest. She half resisted, then grinned back and took it. He tried to chew slowly and enjoy the remains of his mouthful, as he watched her close her eyes and relish every last bit of juice and fruit. They shared the rest of it, each being careful to only have a fair share. Too quickly it was gone.

"That was the best, the best ever. Thank you for waiting to share it." He felt so much better and before he could say more Wolvzzar was calling them to begin again.

Boy had no idea of whether it was day or night or how long they had been walking when Wolvzzar suddenly stopped and sniffed the air.

"There is water here. Not too far away. Come."
He was thirsty again and his spirits rose at the thought of a long drink. It had been so hot in the stale air, but now the temperature was dropping. There was a breeze against his face. The pack began to hurry. There was a noise, a steady roar somewhere in the distance. They continued to climb. The noise became louder and louder. The air became damper, fresher somehow. It was getting brighter, he wasn't relying on Mellana's light anymore. In front of them the steps were wider and wider, leading to an archway from where the light was coming.

The rock around the arch was smooth and covered in runes. In front of the arch was a huge hole in the roof, it seemed to stretch upwards, but was lost in the darkness. The noise interrupted his thoughts. The roaring was increasing.

It was coming from the other side of the archway. Every step it became lighter. What, he wondered was awaiting them?

The wolves bounded ahead and gathered at the top of the stairs. Boy followed them. He gasped in awe as he looked through the archway into a hall. The walls were a mixture of columns, runes and sculptured figures. Large sweeping columns led up to the ceiling, decorated with trees and flowers and creatures. It was strange because the creatures were out of proportion to any trees and flowers he knew. Stalactites hung from the ceiling dropping water onto the flat stone floor. But it was the far wall, that drew everyone's attention.

Boy stared with the wolves. Five arches had been cut through the rock from nearly floor to ceiling. You couldn't see beyond the openings, like giant windows, because blocking the view was a wall of water. A huge waterfall. The noise was deafening.

Boy was thirsty. He ran across the hall, getting wet from the spray as he neared the water and cupped his hand to get a drink. As his hand touched the water, it was slapped downwards by the sheer weight of water. It was icy cold, like being hit by hundreds of tiny needles. He quickly pulled it away. As he rubbed his hand, Boy realised the wolves were gathered by a huge stone on the right-hand side of the hall. Waist high, it was like a giant birdbath, held up by a stone plynth carved into the shape of a hand. He quickly joined them for a cool refreshing drink.

As Boy finished Mellana shouted. She had gone to the far end of the hall. The final archway did not have a water curtain like the others. It was an open archway. The wolves gathered beside her. He stayed, reluctant to leave the cool refreshing water, splashing it over his face and savouring the sweet taste.

"There. It's there."

The wolves had crowded round her and he heard Wolvzzar say,

"Yes, child you are right." The relief and pleasure in his voice were obvious.

Boy ran over to them, squirmed passed the shifting legs of the wolves and pushed up by Mellana. She grabbed him, beaming.

"Look, look. You can see it."

From the open archway there were steps leading down against the rock face and away from the waterfall.

He looked up above the steps. The rock face seemed to go up forever. Downwards, it carried on down, thousands of steps, that eventually went into a forest. They were hundreds of metres up above it. Then he realised what she had meant. For across the forest canopy, many, many kilometres away in the far distance he could see, a mountain. Cone shaped. On its own. Snow-capped upon grey rock.

But there, beneath the grey rock, around its base, he could make out a band of purple and yellow. The purple mountain. Their goal. They had found it.

Chapter 12 - The Jungle and Beyond

He stared up at the gorge cliff and shook his head. He dared not try and climb back up now night time had fallen. The descent into the gorge had been hard. Harder than he had expected. One horse lost, the last of the spare ones. He had whipped the man, to remind them to be careful. Any lost horse from now on, was a man lost.

But tonight, was for rest and a long soak in the shallow river. He would let the men enjoy the water.

It could be tomorrow they catch up with the wolf pack. He wanted the men fresh for the battle.

Before the descent, the tracker had showed him the marks the wolves had left. The wolves had apparently lingered near the top of the cliff. A day and night the tracker thought. Why? Two children. Why? He would need to find out before he killed them.

The screeching birds. Yes, they would need to take extra care.

* * *

The sighting of the purple mountain and the refreshing water, meant all the hardships were forgotten. Mellana hugged Boy and he hugged her back. The wolves were moving around excitedly, pushing each other and the children in their joy.

Wolvzzar called them to order and they gathered near the stone bowl. They stood in a circle facing one another.

Together they intoned the Prophesy:

When sickness is all around you,
journey west for the valley on high.
There you must look for an entrance
on a path that is hidden from sight.

Search for a sign so familiar
and enter the door in the light.
It will take you on a journey of danger
by steps that are dark but give hope.

Seek a mountain of yellow and purple
through creatures terrible to see.
Harvest the goodness that grows there
to save those at home who may die.

Yet only one on two legs can help you,
and only one who carries our sign.
Guide him, for he will be cub like,
in need of your speed and your fangs.

For the sake of the packs protect him,
give him time to learn and understand
that within him is the power to aid you,
in this dark and most dangerous of times.'

Wolvzzar addressed them.

"It is indeed the time of the Prophesy. We have all seen the signs and the power in Boy. I do not think there can be any doubt that our belief in the Prophesy and in you Boy, is justified."

Boy didn't know what to say. He just wished he would not go quite so red when he was being looked at. But it did feel good to be praised by Wolvzzar even if it was in front of others.

Wolvzzar continued.

"It will take you on a journey to danger
by steps that are dark but give hope

Seek a mountain of yellow and purple
through creatures terrible to see."

He stopped, looked at each wolf and child in turn.

"I fear the journey in front of us will be full of dangers. We must be watchful of everything we see or touch. We will need to take care and yet," he paused, "we must make haste wherever we can. Come let us make our packs proud and deliver them from this sickness. Run long, run safe, run for the pack."

The other Wolves nodded their approval and intoned in reply.

"Run long, run safe, run for the pack."

Wolvzzar led them through the archway to the steps. Thousands upon thousands of steps, cut into the rock and leading down into a forest.

He signalled they should descend, warning them to keep close to the rock face. For at the other side of the steps was a drop too deep to contemplate.

Boy followed the wolves out, stopping to take one more look around and wonder who had created this hall and why. He puzzled at the carvings of men and the waterfall that surrounded three stones that had been set into the wall. The stones, were square in shape, about the size of his hand, and had wavy vertical lines carved into them. The three stones were set between each of the columns. Then Byter was nudging him forward and he focused on what lay ahead.

The steps, like those in the tunnel were old and worn and must have been cut out many, many years ago. Within a few steps the atmosphere changed completely. It was like walking into a wall of humid heat. It was relieved to a degree by the constant cool spray from the waterfall beside and above him. Below him the forest trees weren't like home or Chylgar. They were like pictures of a jungle. A tangle of huge green leaves and long vine ropes hung like tendrils from the treetops, the heat, the noise, the birds and animal cries, roars and shrieks.

The wolves were looking up into the sky, Boy instinctively followed their gaze. Nothing. No, not true, high, high above were birds gliding. They were too far away to be sure if they were the same birds as before. But they were big, of that he was sure. Wolvzzar called for them all to hurry in case it was them. One of the wolves turned and motioned that Byter should go ahead, then himself and Fleetfoot last. He smiled at the wolf. Boy didn't know him well. He kept himself to himself.

Boy then concentrated, for he had to work hard to keep up and so had little time to look at the rich green trees below that seemed to stretch out into the far distance. He could hear the roar of the huge waterfall behind him. He slowed and risked a glance back and up and saw that the waterfall was truly huge. It seemed to stretch all along the mountain wall and beyond it. The rock face curved round and was lost. He tried to see the top of the falls, but it was so high, and the mist from the water made it difficult to see what was above the waterfall.

He would have liked to have stopped and taken it all in, but a growl from Fleetfoot reminded him of the need to keep up. Wolvzzar was rushing, all the time watching out for danger. Boy was struggling to keep up and soon the three of them were beginning to lag behind.

It came out of nowhere. He became aware of a shadow. Almost immediately it was a huge shadow. Boy flattened himself against the rock wall. It was there. A giant bird, sweeping along the wall side, flying on its side, talons outstretched, mouth wide open, rows of razor-sharp teeth now clearly visible. Fleetfoot turned to fight it. There was a thump as the talons caught him mid-body. A cry of pain and he was gone, gone. The giant bird screeched its success as it flew off into the distance, with the wolf hanging limply from its claws.

It had all happened so fast. Boy had had no time to protect him. The pack stood still shocked and dismayed. One of the wolves began to howl. A cry of sorry and loss. Another one joined in before Wolvzzar, snapped at them to stop.

"Where there is one, there will be others. There will be time to mourn our loss later. Boy, go to the middle and ride Byter. Mellana on Growler. Boy, search the skies to stop them. We must hurry. We cannot fight them."

Boy's brain was numb. He should have been watching. He hadn't seen them. Fleetfoot had lost his life for him. The wolves were running down the steps, covering the ground three, four times faster than before. The constant jolts made him cling on to Byter's fur. He felt his eyes watering. *It's my fault!* was all he could think of. He felt the sadness of the pack around him. A voice came into his mind. It was Wolvzzar.

"*You are not responsible. Feel the sadness of our loss, but only that. It is the way. You must not blame yourself Boy. Help us now. Use your sharp eyes and help protect us my child.*"

"*Yes Wolvzzar.*" Boy looked up and started to scan the skies above him. At first it was a speck in the distance. Then it became a bird circling a long way away. Then it was two, three no half a dozen.

"Wolvzzar, they are gathering," shouted Boy to all the wolves.

The pack did not slow to look. The forest canopy was getting nearer. Boy had to keep wiping the sweat from his eyes so he could see. The sun was dazzling. He could feel the white-hot power building inside him. Then saw that the birds had moved. They had gone. The sky was clear. It didn't make sense. He grabbed Byter so he could turn and look behind him.

"Look Byter! There!" he pointed furiously. "There they are, just above the forest. There must be two, no three of them." Silent this time, rushing towards them, skimming the canopy he watched them swerve to come to the rock wall behind him, then twist like fighter planes so they were vertical, flying along the wall, towards them.

He thought of the beautiful wolf lost trying to protect him, felt the anger and power grow. He felt the jolting of Byter running down the steps, gasped as he slipped towards the wall, felt the graze on his arm. Felt the pain. Felt the anger, pain and power. He was ready. He would make them pay.

"I hate you," he screamed. "Why don't you die!" He lashed out, jabbing at them as he spoke. Then gasped as the first bird, screeched in pain, its feathers alight. Its whole body on fire. The second and third birds too close, crashed into it, smashing against the rock, spinning out of control, falling out of the sky. Spinning slowly now, as if in slow motion, smoke trailing behind them, they disappeared into the forest canopy below.

Boy looked around, others were coming. Except this time, the anger had gone. He was confused. Had the power drained away? They were coming from below, their talons outstretched. Fear and panic rose in him. '*No,*' his mind shouted. The lead bird screeched surprise and peeled away, the ones behind it followed its lead.

They circled and started to return. Again, his order to go and this time, they turned and screeching defiance, flapped their wings furiously and flew away across the tree tops.

Chapter 13 - The Forest

"Spears up. Control that horse, soldier. Here they come again!"

The Captain looked around, desperately seeking a way out. The men shouting, the screams of the terrified horses, the bone chilling screech of the birds.

The birds. He had never seen such creatures. They came out of nowhere. Giant killer birds. They had taken two men and horses already. There had to be a way out. He looked around wildly. The light was in his eyes, he could barely see the birds against the brilliance of the rising sun.

His heart leapt.

"Look. All of you. Behind us. That shadow on the wall. It's a tunnel opening. Back up, quickly towards it. It must be where they went. Look out! They are circling lower again! Quickly! Before they attack again."

* * *

They were near the forest canopy. The heat was worse. The rock wall was dripping with moisture from the clinging mold. It was the noise though. Birds, animals. Boy had no idea what they were. There was rustling in the tree tops near them. Bird? Animal? He couldn't tell. The leaves, and giant ferns, meant he couldn't see what it was. They were still descending and he clung onto Byter tightly. Boy realised the trees had to be huge, for the pack was still high up. Giant vines hung down from many trees. He could just see the brown jungle floor far beneath them.

He was still in a state of shock. Remembering the loss of Fleetfoot, he took comfort from being on Byter's back. He was also thinking about the bird bursting into flames. He knew he had done that. But how? What was this power, this thing he had? If he could do that, what else could he do? He needed to talk to Wolvzzar. Byter slipped slightly and Boy became aware that the pack had stopped.

All the wolves were sniffing the air. They were talking about the smells and trying to decide if there was any immediate danger. They sensed there were mostly small animals around them. Byter assured Boy, they could tell the difference between the scent of small prey and large beasts, even if the creatures were strange to them. But there were other smells. Predator smells. Old but there. They would need to take care.

They continued down the steps. The jungle was so rich in colours now they were nearer to the jungle floor. So many different shades of green. Bushes with flowers of deep reds and purples. The ground now clearer. Dark brown. In places covered with lush grasses. To the right, a half-fallen tree, creating an impenetrable screen. To the left a small clearing, light flowing in from it.

Wolvzzar froze as a deep roar came from behind the screen. In the distance, but who knew how far away.

Byter turned to Growler and whispered to Mellana and Boy.

"Whatever it is, it is not hunting. It is a territory cry. It fears little. The wind is coming towards us. It cannot smell us. Be still, very still."

The roar again, but this time louder. It was moving towards them. They could hear it now, brushing through the undergrowth. Snuffling sounds as it tasted the different smells around it. Boy felt Byter tensing his muscles beneath him, saw Wolvzzar, Hunnta and the others lower their backs, so they could spring forward at the animal. His mouth felt dry. The rustling stopped, the sniffing of the air louder. Boy realised in horror that it had to be on the other side of the fallen tree. His mouth opened. Through the upper branches of the fallen tree, he could see a grey shape. The top of its back. It was massive.

"*Use your power Boy,*" said Wolvzzar's voice. Boy felt panic rising. There was nothing there. He didn't feel calm or angry. He didn't feel the build up inside him. He just felt scared. It was so big. He was sure it must be much bigger than an elephant even. Perhaps twice as big.

The creature suddenly went silent. It started to turn. Its back was sideways to them. He heard it snort and then through the branches of the fallen tree, a spray like a hose. A massive hose, of yellow not clear water. It was peeing he thought. He couldn't stop himself laughing, held his hand to his mouth. He felt the fear drain away. The laughter wouldn't stop. It was the biggest pee in the world, he thought.

Then it had stopped. The snuffling amongst the forest started and the rustling and growling. It was going away. Boy's stomach was hurting. The relief, the craziness. He collapsed onto Byter's back and stayed there, arms locked around his neck. Boy felt Byter relax and hang his head for a second and then shake it.

"The jungle. The bird. Fleetfoot Now this giant of a creature. Boy, I do wonder what sort of land we have entered."

"Before we move." Wolvzzar said. "Let us for a moment remember Fleetfoot. He gave his life for Boy and the pack. He will be remembered in our Tales of Glory at the coming together of the Clan."

There was a rumbling of agreement.

"For now, we must be on our guard. Hunnta, you and Sylvabak must scout the land for us when we move. Smorlears will cover our rear. At night we will have a guard at all times." He sighed. "This forest is full of unknown dangers, BUT," he looked up and round, "this journey has already been too long. We cannot tarry. We must be as swift as we dare."

Hunnta, Smorlears and Sylvabak disappeared from view, quickly followed by Wolvzzar and the pack. Boy and Mellana remained on the backs of their wolves. They could not afford to risk any delays. The wolves were running through the forest, jumping over branches, swerving around trees and bushes. Initially Boy concentrated on hanging on as Byter turned this way and that, but the days of riding now meant he quickly adjusted to this new way of running.

He settled into the rhythm and his mind started to wander. He looked around whenever he could risk it. The trees and bushes, the shape of the trees. All new to him and yet familiar. Boy felt himself go cold. He remembered. This was the scene from his dream. The scene he had partially relived when Detra was hurt.

What if the dream was to repeat itself? Would it be a dream? Would there be danger there? He wanted to say something. But what? Wouldn't he sound silly? What was he to tell them they shouldn't do? Boy knew in his heart he should say something. Perhaps at the next break. They had been going some time. Byter and Growler would need to stop soon surely.

His mind was swirling with thoughts. He wanted to have the chance to talk to Mellana. Enough had happened now for her at least to take him seriously. She could advise him. Yes, he realised, that was the answer.

Just then Hunnta called back for them to slow. They gathered quietly and traced their way around a huge bush that was blocking their path. There, still, perfectly still, stood Hunnta and Sylvabak. They were watching something.

"Deer," said Hunnta quietly. "Look through the bush and see."

Byter and the others crept up and gazed through the less bushy parts. Boy saw a herd of deer. Maybe twenty, thirty. It was difficult to see. But the deer were not like those at home. Because they were as tall as Byter. They were huge. At that point, there was a snort from the other side of the herd.

It was the stag. Its eyes looked around, checking for danger, sensing something wrong. The female deer parted and Boy could see it properly as he moved nearer the bush. He was even bigger. Bigger than Hunnta. The massive set of antlers had pointed prongs that faced out at any attacker. Around its head and hind quarters was thick skin, like armour plating, in segments so it could move easily. The thick skin merged into a fine fur around its middle. But running along its back, all the way to its stumpy tail, were short horns, curved towards it rear.

"It would take the whole pack to bring such a beast down," whispered Byter. Then Boy heard him wonder in awe. "So why does he need such protection. How big are the hunters here?"

Boy felt a chill run through him as he realised what Byter meant. The giant birds. Oversized trees and deer. A land of giants where even the wolves may not be able to protect him. He felt very afraid.

"We must stay calm," Wolvzzar directed. He turned away and the others followed. At a safe distance, he gathered them together.

"It is as I feared. There is great danger here. We must learn to be the hunted, as well as the hunters. Sylvabak lead us around the deer, I do not wish to draw attention to ourselves."

Boy looked across at Mellana. Saw his own worries reflected in her face. He half-smiled, but before he could think of anything to say, Sylvabak and Hunnta had leapt forward and Byter and the others were following. As they carried on, he frowned. He had forgotten to tell Wolvzzar about the dream.

.

Chapter 14 - The Mountain of Purple and Yellow

The captain felt his frustration growing with every step. The horses had to be walked up the steps. This tunnel staircase was costing them precious time. The wolves would be fleeter than his horses. He was sure they were losing time. So much effort made to catch them and now this!

"Perhaps we should wait here Captain. We could set traps for them. They have to come back this way don't they."

The Sergeant looked nervous. Making suggestions the Captain didn't like could end up with a whipping. But he was exhausted and the chance to stop was not to be wasted.

"Perhaps Sergeant, you should concentrate on doing what I say. Stopping is not a good idea. How do we know this is the only route? We don't know why they are on this journey. Only that it must be essential for the pack. And," he gripped the soldier by the throat, "does it not occur to you Sergeant, that the most obvious reason for their journey is to bring back more packs of wolves? Who would be trapped then, eh? Fool." He sneered at the Sergeant and turned away.

"Move, we have wasted enough time."

* * *

"We need to rest soon and I sense water," said Wolvzzar. Boy's unease was growing. This forest was looking more and more like the one in his dream. He needed to speak to Wolvzzar now, it couldn't wait.

"Wolvzzar," Boy called, heart in his mouth. "Please, can we stop for a moment, I need to say something." Wolvzzar halted the pack and came back to him. Every step seemed to take an age and Boy was already regretting saying anything.

"Well, tell me Boy. What is it that it is so urgent that we must stop." Byter grumbled underneath him and he caught Mellana's puzzled expression. He was tongue tied. He couldn't say it. It would sound so stupid.

"I. I thought I saw something. Sorry Wolvzzar. I made a mistake," he stammered looking away.

When he looked back, Wolvzzar was still staring at him. The wolf's eyes seemed to shut out everything. They filled his vision.

"Tell me."

Boy realised he had no choice. He quietly explained. He told him of the dream where he had first met Wolvzzar. Of the run and how alike the area was. How he worried that if they came to such a stream it was important. Danger he thought.

Growler snorted. "Can't this wait." Wolvzzar looked at Growler.

"No, it is well he wanted to protect us." He turned back to Boy.

"Yes, I came to you in the dream. Yes, I sensed you in your world. But I do not understand this fear. Or if it is a fear or something else. Rest easy for we shall be on our guard." He put his head on one side for a minute and then summoned them. "Come pack. We rest soon."

Boy felt relieved he had spoken, but knew there was more to it.

"I sense water," said Byter. "Can you smell it Boy?" Boy sniffed the air. There were so many scents and smells, almost assaulting his nose, he had no way of recognising the gentle scent of water.

"No, but I am so thirsty it would be good to stop and drink."

"I would not disagree Boy, for you may look slimmer, but in truth I am sure you do not get any lighter."
Boy laughed apologetically and stroked his back.

"Sorry Byter."

Before he knew it, Hunnta was calling for them to stop. They were at the edge of the clearing. It was exactly like the clearing in his dream. The size of the clearing, the stream, the mist rising. He had thought it was evening mist in the dream, but here it was a heat mist.

The only difference was that a tree had fallen. Slimmer than most, it had fallen a third of the way across the clearing. It had few branches and they were close to the trunk, so he could still see across the whole area. The wolves carefully moved to the edge.

Boy leaned forward towards Byter's head. He didn't want anyone else to hear.

"It is the clearing. The clearing in my dreams. I'm sure of it," he whispered defiantly. "Apart from that fallen tree, it is the same."

"I sense no danger," Byter replied. "Let us trust Wolvzzar. I am sure it is safe. At the moment." He continued to look around.

"We will water and rest for the night near the trees." Wolvzzar said. "Grapors and Runlong, stand guard whilst we drink."

Boy didn't know what to do. He knew this was the clearing. It made no sense that the two should be the same. But he was sure.

The pack drank and then returned to the edge of clearing where they could rest and be hidden. There was little conversation. They felt the loss of Fleetfoot. They knew they were going to have to cross this dangerous jungle, only to return. There were few happy thoughts around the pack.

A noise. Something moving in the jungle.

Byter hissed to Boy and Mellana,

"Stand behind me. There is something out there. It is big. It moves without effort to disguise its presence. Only one who fears little acts like this!"

As one, the pack moved into the forest undergrowth and hid from view. Boy and Mellana exchanged worried glances. Everyone was still. Boy felt Byter's breath on his neck, felt the reassurance of his presence so close to him.

The noise grew. A growl. Dark and deep and loud.

"Look Boy," whispered Mellana, nudging him to look across the clearing. The bushes were moving. He strained to see through the leaves. They moved again. He felt Byter tense.

Then it was there. It was coming out of the bushes. Green and brown. Bigger than the wolves. Much bigger. And broader. Like a giant cat. But with massive paws. It curled back its mouth to reveal viscous looking pointed teeth. It stopped half way out of the bushes and roared again. It looked around, sniffed the air. It continued towards the water. Leisurely, graceful but huge and deadly.

Boy could only stare. It halted, sniffing the air. It was looking around and then focused its gaze in their direction. It dropped its head, still looking straight across the clearing to where they were hidden. Its eyes, so large. Cold and hard. The wolves shifted in alarm. It must have spotted them.

Boy could barely breath. He felt the fear and power begin to gather within him. He could save them. He would save them. He was sure. He focused everything on the Giant cat. '*No!*' He commanded in his mind. '*Go back.*'

The beast stopped mid stride. Put its head to one side. A voice in his head. A voice of authority. Like Wolvzzar but different. Not Wolvzzar's. Harder and colder in tone. One word. " *Why?*" It said in his mind. Then continued towards them.

Boy panicked. He felt the power. Why didn't it stop the creature? It spoke though. And to him. It must know he is there! All he could think of was repeating the command. '*Stop.*' He wanted to shout it out loud. The giant cat ignored him, just continued its slow and steady walk towards them, its eyes now fixed on him. Boy could not think. What could he do? It would kill them all. "*I can't stop it Wolvzzar,*" he said in his mind.

It reached the fallen tree and started to step over it. Then suddenly the small branches on the tree flattened. The end of the tree, that went into the bushes reared. It had a head, a snake's head. The other end near the stream, rose. It was the snake's tail. It wasn't a tree at all, it was a monster sized snake. Almost quicker than the eye could follow, it curled around the giant cat. The snake's head, huge, as big as Byter's. Its jaws opened as it swung up and above the giant cat. Lightning fast.

The giant cat realising the danger, turned its head to face the snake. Too late, the snake's head dived down, its massive jaws and fangs biting and holding the back of the giant cat's neck. The giant cat screamed its pain. The coils continued to wrap around it. The giant cat half turned and raked the snake's body with its claws. Blood poured from the snake's side. Its coils tightened.

It was horrible to watch. Boy couldn't watch it.

'*No.*' He shouted in his head. "Stop." This time out loud. The wolves, startled, jumped to one side. Boy was now focused on the snake. It released its grip. Blood poured from its wound. It reared up in confusion.

"Go!" Boy commanded, his arms out-stretched, palms up facing the snake, as he walked steadily into the clearing. The snake backed away, uncoiling from the injured giant cat's body. Still rearing up, it slithered backwards and away into the forest.

The giant cat lay on its side, panting. It lifted its head and then gradually got up. Blood covered its neck where the snake had bitten it. The same word. This time the voice, forced and in pain, questioning. "*Why?*" The huge beast slowly turned and painfully walked to the stream. It lay by the bank and lapped up some water.

Boy began to walk slowly towards the wounded animal. There was a movement and rustling behind him and then he felt Mellana just behind him. Byter called out to them, but then he heard Wolvzzar's quiet command.

"Let them go."

Boy did not understand why he was doing this. He felt his heart thumping. His legs were wooden and yet he knew. He knew he had to go and took heart that Mellana had grown to trust his instincts.

The walk to the water's edge seemed to last forever. Each step seemed to pound in his ears. He saw the giant cat turn to watch them, while resting its head on its paws. Boy reached it.

The giant cat looked at him, with eyes that seemed to take him in and understand all of him, before its gaze shifted to Mellana, who had bent down to the water's edge and was soaking his old jumper in the water. She stood and reached up, to wipe the fur and wound. It flinched and growled, half turning, then returned to rest its head on its paws again. Mellana stopped, then continued to wipe the blood away.

Boy stretched out his arm, trying hard to keep it from shaking and placed his hand on its back. He became aware of the luxuriant feel of its fur under his hands. He felt it shivering, but he was also aware of the muscles and strength there. Mellana ripped the jumper into two and pointed to the other side of the beast. Nodding, Boy took the bloodied cloth and washed it out before walking slowly round to begin cleaning the other side.

When they had done, the giant cat lurched to its feet. It looked deep into Boy's eyes. The eyes. They held him as completely as any chain. He felt their strength and power. The voice again. This time calmer. Considered.

"*Our paths will cross again. I will remember this day.*" It slowly and painfully turned and walked away across the clearing, away from the wolves.

Boy stood there. Wet jumper in hand, watching him go. The wolves slowly came out from the bushes. No one knew quite what to say.

Boy turned to Mellana.

"Thank you. It was very brave of you to come with me."

She smiled. "It was the right thing to do and I trust your power." He didn't know how to answer and worried at the responsibility.

The wolves were forming a semicircle around him. Before he could speak Wolvzzar stepped forward.

"This gift Boy. It is beyond my knowledge. That you saved the pack and the journey from ruin is in no doubt."

He stopped and considered for a moment. "I sense you were right Boy. That gesture may be important one day."

Boy looked up into Wolvzzar's eyes.

"It spoke to me though. I just knew I had to." He shrugged his shoulders because he didn't understand why he did it. Only that he had to.

The wolves turned to Wolvzzar.

"I heard no voice." said Wolvzzar quietly. He nodded, clearly thinking. "Then Perhaps your gesture was both brave and important. Today we cannot know. Hunnta, Sylvabak, check both the snake and injured hunter have moved away." He looked up at the darkening skies. "Let us rest, the best we can."

Neither Mellana or Boy were really hungry and both chewed without enthusiasm on their food.

"Boy," asked Mellana. "What did his voice sound like?"

Boy frowned. "It was deep and kinda scary. Like Wolvzzar but dark and hard somehow." He shrugged his shoulders. Mellana studied him thoughtfully.

"So, can you hear all the animals talk. Can you listen in? Are all the noises, voices to you?"

"No, I don't control who or what I hear. It just happens. I couldn't talk to the snake, just tell it to stop. It is only Wolvzzar and the wolves and now the beast."

Mellana thought for a second. "So, can you talk to animals in your world?"

"I don't think so. Wolvzzar was the first animal I have ever spoken to."

The questions ran out for now. They went quiet and soon Byter joined them and together they settled for the night. Somehow Boy wasn't sleepy and he lay there for a while, listening to the night creatures and thinking about the beast and its power. About how he could control the snake, but not the giant cat. He also wondered what it meant when it said *"Our paths will cross again. I will remember this day."*

It had been a long day and found himself drifting whilst wondering what would happen next.

Chapter 15 - But What are They?

The horses drank greedily as the Captain stood, arms crossed looking out at the jungle. He had no idea how much time they had lost. The forest below them was a blow. It would be hard work to catch them in this terrain. The steps would also be difficult for the horses again. And birds can fly over mountains. He would have to keep one eye on the sky.

"Sergeant, time to move."

* * *

The next day the pack continued to run. It was exhausting. Every sound to be listened to, every movement to be double checked. Nothing to be trusted. Snakes that could so cleverly disguise themselves and predators the size of the giant cat, were warnings of what could lie ahead.

By evening, Byter and Growler were tired beyond measure. Mellana and Boy could not run, it was too dangerous. In turn, they were both sore and weary. Again, the staff practice was put aside and they quickly lay down to sleep, against the already sleeping form of Byter.

Boy woke early the next day. His sleep had been deep and dreamless. He lay against the warmth and softness of Byter's fur. His head and body moving with Byter's breathing. He leaned forward, stretched and looked around. The others were still sleeping. Other than Hunnta and

Sylvabak, the two wolves keeping watch. They acknowledged Boy but then ignored him as they kept guard.

A new sound made him look up. It was a bird. A large bird, with a plumage of reds and yellows and the deepest purples. It was breathtakingly beautiful. Its call was so tuneful. He watched as it opened its purple and white wings and flew to the next tree, away from the camp. Entranced, he followed it, only a few metres, the wolves were still quite close. It became aware of him. It ceased its call, looked down and then flew two trees away to begin its song all over again.

He started to follow and then stopped. In front of him was a patch of thick reedy grass, as tall as him. In the middle was a flower of such beauty. He had never been much for flowers and had no interest in his Dad's garden but this was different. The flower head had to be three feet wide. Two giant petals, one above the other. They were red and yellow and green. Between the petals, four small fruits swayed. They looked so tasty. Like strawberries but redder and more succulent looking.

He wondered. Perhaps if he picked one and sniffed it. That could do no harm. It didn't seem dangerous here. He licked his lips. He was so thirsty and the sweet perfume tempted him. He lent forward and was just about to touch it, when he heard Wolvzzar's command. In his head.

'*Stop. Fool! Do not move.*'

He stood stock still, his arm outstretched. What was behind him? Seconds passed. Nothing. Where were they? Where was the danger? Boy felt his arm beginning to ache but didn't dare move. He didn't know how long he would be able to hold this position. What could the danger be? It had to be something behind him.

He gathered himself, ready to leap into the reeds for cover. Then he heard a rustling behind. What kind of animal? He got ready to launch himself, when he felt a large stick brush passed his head. It hit the flower and the two petals instantly folded back to reveal rows of teeth. The petals or mouth snapped together crushing the stick and disappearing into the reeds. Byter grabbed his arm and threw him to the ground away from the reeds, just as the head reappeared, jaws gaping and slammed shut, exactly where he had been standing. Shaken and bruised, he slowly stood up to find himself looking into Byter's angry face.

"When will you learn that it is not just your own foolish life you risk, but those of our families, the sick and dying at home."

Byter turned away before he could say anything. Boy's face was burning. He felt so stupid and frightened.

Mellana came up, and just looked him. Then she shook her head and grimacing, squeezed his arm and put her hand on his shoulders.

They walked back slowly.

Boy knew he should say something. But he felt sick, realising how close he had been to being killed. He also hated the fact Byter had shouted at him.

"Thank you, Byter. I'm sorry."

"You frighten me Boy." He said in a now calm voice. "You are like a pack leader one moment, a young cub the next." He gently pushed his head into Boy's back, nudging him towards the camp. "It is as well Mellana knows how to throw that stick of hers."

"It was a great throw." Boy smiled at Mellana. "I can't believe a flower could be that deadly."

"Well you haven't done too bad so far. Although that was pretty stupid." She started to giggle and he started to laugh too. Then Byter was wheezing his laughter. They both leaned against Byter as he walked between them, relief suddenly overwhelming all three of them. The pack wolves looked in disbelief as they walked into camp laughing still.

Wolvzzar called them over. He waited without expression as they tried to be serious.

"I know nothing more needs to be said. But for all our sakes Boy," he bent down to within an inch of Boy's face, "you will not wander off again, will you?"

"No Wolvzzar." He felt ashamed but still looked up quizzically. "How did you know it was dangerous?"

Wolvzzar sighed. "The fault is partly ours. There was a feel of death around those reeds. We should have told you. There are so many dangers here to be watchful of. Well done Byter."

Byter nodded, clearly pleased that Wolvzzar had acknowledged his role.

After a quick cold breakfast, they set off again. As Boy climbed onto Byter, he leaned towards his ear.

"Thank you for saving my life."

"Next time it will be me that bites your head off," the wolf retorted.

"I promise Byter, never again. I was sure it was safe. I thought I was beginning to learn. I shall be more careful. Promise."

They ran for the rest of the morning, slowing only when they could feel a rumble of feet or a loud noise that meant a large animal of some sort. Boy noticed it was getting lighter in front of them, he couldn't make sense of it. Before he could say anything, they had burst out into sunshine and fields. The ground in front of them a gentle slope down, towards the rolling hills that stretched out in front of them.

The wolves were not looking at the hills. They were staring as one at a grey mass at the base of the long slope.

"What is it, Byter? I can't make it out this far away."

"Animals. It is a herd of some sort. But I have never seen such animals. I think they are eating grass."
There were quiet growls of agreement.

"I agree, they are grass eaters," said Wolvzzar. "We can probably go around them, without going too far from our path." He signaled that was his intention and they set off down the grassy banks.

The air smelt so much cleaner here and with the gentle breeze, so much less humid than in the jungle. Wolvzzar was taking them to the left of the herd, and gradually he could make out more detail. They were full bodied, with triangular shaped horns that ran down the whole of their back and the length of their thick tail. They had long, thick necks. It meant they could eat the grass without bending forward. The heads were plated in armour with horns on top. He watched with amazement.

As they ran along nearing the herd, it began to dawn on Boy, why the wolves had been so astonished. It was their size. They were huge. They were as big as a two-storey house.

The lead ones had stopped eating to watch the wolves and had clearly decided they were no threat. But at that point the lead one turned, looked behind the wolves and bellowed. The whole herd started bellowing and closing in on itself.

Without anything being said between them, the pack immediately increased its pace. Boy felt Byter's speed and had to concentrate on staying on. Soon the pack was in full flight.

Boy felt the familiar tightening and churning in his stomach. Something was very wrong. He gripped Byter harder with his hands and legs and leant down low. He was being jolted and banged as Byter sprinted along with the others. The ground was rushing past so fast, he knew it would be very painful if he fell off. What was it that could make the pack take flight?

Then he heard it. A roar. So loud it made his ears hurt. A roar that sent his blood cold. Yet he dare not turn as the wolves streaked down the long hill. The thumping. It wasn't his heart. It came from whatever was behind him. The roar again and distressed bellows from the herd.

Wolvzzar was slowing and turning. As Byter swung round he was able to see the herd, crowding together, jostling each other. Beyond them, moving steadily and determinedly towards them, was a monster of a hunter.

Its large long head leaning forward, its giant beak now open to reveal rows of deadly teeth. Its two leathery grey front legs and claws, held out in front of it. The thick muscled, grey body, held upright on its two massive rear legs. Its long thick tail swished backward and forward. He now understood the flight of the wolves. For when it stood upright, it was even bigger than the herd animals.

Wolvzzar did not wait to see what would happen. As one they turned and ran, the roars and bellows of the beast and herd gradually diminishing. Now it was a controlled run, not flight, eyes and ears watchful for other predators. Although the immediate danger was past, Boy remained frightened. He knew for sure he was in a world where even these giants of wolves could not protect him. A world of true monsters.

The purple mountain grew ever closer as they ran up and down the rolling hills. Often the valleys contained woods. Always they moved around them, fearful of what they may contain. Boy and Mellana were fascinated by the many giant creatures that roamed the countryside. Some grass eating giants on two legs, others like giant rhinos. They weaved and dodged to avoid drawing their attention.

Little was said as they halted for the night. Once again, the darkness was filled with strange noises and movements. Boy slept fitfully, constantly worried about what could blunder into their camp. But the end was in sight. The purple haze growing nearer. Now had a new worry. What was he supposed to do once they got there? The words of the Prophesy kept playing through his head.

Earlier that evening Byter had reminded Boy again of the Prophesy when he stood looking at the mountain in the evening light, watching it catch the last of the sun's rays.

'Seek a mountain of yellow and purple
through creatures terrible to see.
Harvest the goodness that grows there
to save those at home who may die.

Yet only one on two legs can help you,
and only one who carries our sign.'

That night he felt as if he had barely slept, tossing and turning. It was still dark when he felt hot breath near his face. It was Byter.

"Why are you so restless Boy? Are you ill?"

"It's the Prophesy. The bit you repeated last night, I don't understand it Byter." He sat up. "What am I supposed to do? What goodness? I know I will let you down."

Byter turned towards Boy and nudged his face with his.

"You have proved you have powers already. Powers I have never heard tell of and never before seen. They will be there for you. I am sure. We are all sure."

Mellana had woken too and was listening to them.

"He's right Boy." She touched his arm in reassurance. "We know you don't know what to do, but each time you have needed to help us, you have." She smiled at him. "It will be okay, I'm sure."

"Yes, but feeling the power is one thing. This goodness. What goodness and am I supposed to find it or do something with it?"

"That, we will find out once we are there. The Prophesy has held true so far has it not? Then let us wait and not seek answers where none can be found." It was Wolvzzar. "You have done well my son. And now you must try and go back to sleep. The mountain beckons and I would be there soon."

Boy tried to sleep, but he knew he couldn't. He felt exhausted when they rose. Breakfast and the warmth of the sun revived him though. They continued to see strange creatures. Some plant eaters had long necks and tails with what looked like plates of bone, like dinner plates, all along their backs. One had a large body, but a tiny head. It was standing on two legs whilst its front legs leaned against a tree trunk, so it could reach the higher leaves.

Fortunately, the only dangerous looking beasts had been moving along in the distance, well away from the pack. At midday they rested by the edge of a small wood. Boy was exhausted from running and the lack of sleep, but equally glad for the exercise to clear his head. He idly watched Hunnta at the furthest corner of the wood, keeping a look out for predators. He was just returning to the pack when Boy saw him freeze.

What had he seen? Then he felt the ground tremble. It got worse. A noise, like a deep rumble in the distance somewhere. It was closing. It was on the other side of the wood. Other noises now. Snorts and bellows. A herd of something. The vibration through the ground was getting stronger. A big herd of big animals. The pack moved backwards and forwards. Wolvzzar and Sylvabak rushed to join Hunnta to see what and where the danger was. They quickly returned and ordered everyone back.

As Boy moved with the pack away from the noise, he turned and he saw them. They were about the same size as the herd animals they had seen before. Huge with thick elephant like legs and bodies. They had a single massive plate, covering the whole of their neck and top of the back. Three horns on their foreheads, two long and a third smaller one on the nose. Instead of a mouth, a vicious looking beak. The animals were passing the edge of the wood, going away from them.

The herd was large, twenty or thirty strong, Boy couldn't be sure. But the vibration, the noise, the dust, it was almost too much. As they passed, he gaped with wonder at their size and shape. They were amazing. Boy, Mellana and the wolves stood very still and waited. Yes, they would be okay. He began to feel the tension drain away

The last one lumbered by. Boy breathed a sigh of relief. But for no reason, the creature looked around. It stopped, saw them and let out a great bellow to the other herd members. Gradually and almost in slow motion, they turned, caught sight of the pack and moved around to face them.

The first animal was stamping its feet, shaking its head, the vicious giant horns flashing in the sunlight. It was bellowing and bellowing. The noise. One by one they all began to stamp and bellow. Boy's heart was in his mouth.

They were moving. He realised in horror, they were forming a huge ring around the pack, still bellowing, stamping their feet, creating more and more clouds of dust.

As the herd started to close in, the wolves formed a defensive half ring facing them. Snarling, ears back, eyes wide, lips curled.

"Calm everybody. Be ready to turn and run if I say. Byter, Growler, be ready to grab the cubs." Wolvzzar's voice, controlled but urgent. "Boy can you stop them?" Mellana's eyes were wide with horror. They were coming closer. The fearsome horns pointed directly at them.

Boy felt the familiar feeling, but this time something it was different. Yes power, but no anger, no fear. Calm. Yes, he was calm. He knew he could stop them from attacking. He nodded, put out both arms and began walking towards them speaking to the herd animals gently, almost whispering. The one in the middle of the ring, larger than the others, shook his head at Boy, bellowed, dropped his head, and charged. Before he could think, Boy thrust his arm out and gave the "Stop" command. The animal immediately halted. Uncertain what to do, it bellowed its confusion. Boy kept on whispering, now louder and louder to the other animals, telling them to be calm, as you would to a frightened puppy. The ones immediately in front of him, raised their heads, puzzled. Their stamping ceased. Gradually more and more ceased their bellowing and shuffling of feet.

The front ones began to back away. With each step he had to lift his head higher and higher, to keep looking into the eyes of the huge beasts. As he neared them, he became more and more aware of their strong pungent smell. The middle section gave way to him as he walked slowly through. He started to look from side to side as the animals surrounded him. They were so big. He was conscious of them towering above him. The smell so strong, the dust swirling around him.

All Boy could see was a sea of grey bodies and white horns, long and cruel. He focused on their leader.

"Gently, gently. I will not hurt you. Shhhhh. Calm." The animals in front of him stopped retreating. He looked into the small yellow eyes that gazed down at him. He reached out and placed his hand upon the rough but warm top of its beaked mouth. It reared up and bellowed. Shocked by the touch.

"*Be careful, Boy. Do not rush it,*" whispered Wolvzzar in his head. He reached up again, his heart pounding now. He had to carry on. The beast stared at him, then slowly, so slowly, lowered its head towards his hand. He felt its hot breath on his arm. Instead of encouraging it to go, he kept talking, stroking its beak and the leathery side of it head. The creature turned slightly so that the one eye came closer to him.

"Yes," he said, "you will protect us as we travel to the mountain, won't you?" He turned to the herd that surrounded him, felt his control move over them all, like an invisible mist gently enveloping them all.

Boy turned to look back at the wolves and Mellana. No one was moving. He spoke to Wolvzzar in his mind.

"*Follow us. They will protect us to the mountain. Byter can join me. I am sure it will be safe.*" He saw Wolvzzar confer with Byter, He smiled at the thought of what Byter was probably saying. Then Byter slowly and carefully moved towards him. He halted at the edge of the herd, before dropping his head and continuing to Boy's side. Some bellowed as he passed them, others moved about nervously.

"Thank you Byter," Boy whispered as he reached him. "Thank you for your trust."

"I hope you know what you doing Boy. I cannot say I am entirely comfortable being in the middle of a herd of animals that could crush us at any second."

Boy, half-smiled and quickly climbed up. He faced the wall of animals and then Byter slowly moved forward. The animals, bellowed nervously as boy and wolf walked between them. The other wolves with Mellana, initially walked behind and then came through the herd, until the pack had fully reassembled at the front of the herd.

The beasts huge size meant despite their ponderous movements, they could keep up with the loping wolf pace. The wolves spoke little, in awe of their protectors and increasingly seeing Boy for what he was and what he could be.

The cone shaped mountain and the purple and yellow haze were more clearly defined. Now they could also see a ring around the bottom of it. Grey, like a wall. The unlikely procession made good time. Wolvzzar and the pack, relaxing as they began to trust their protectors. A small pack of raptors, that would have been trouble, kept clear of the herd of giants with their vicious looking horns. Later as they passed a lake, the leader entered a bellowing contest with a huge raptor. Faced with so many, the beast quickly retreated.

At sunset. Wolvzzar called a halt. Boy was relieved and exhausted. Keeping the herd in his mind the whole time, controlling them, required immense concentration. That he could retain the power was so different from before. But now he just wanted to stop and let go. He was so tired. Boy slipped off Byter and walked slowly back to the leader. It bent its head. Boy reached up and stroked its beak.

"Thank you. I shall never forget this day. Go now on your journey."

The giant, lifted its head and bellowed gently, calling to the others. Boy quickly got out of the way as they watched the herd thunder away into the darkening evening.

Chapter 16 - The Wall and Beyond

"One man lost and another injured, but he will keep up." The Captain acknowledged the Sergeants report. He wondered if the tracker was right and one of the wolves had been taken by the birds. That would make up for the lost soldiers.

"Was the horse saved?" he asked. The Sergeant nodded. "Good." Horses were valuable, he could not afford to lose more. He had no interest in the soldier that had been killed, just that it depleted his force by one. The injured man, well, as long as he didn't hold them up, he could remain. Otherwise he would be left behind.

He had never seen such a beast though. Big cats he had seen, hunted even. But nothing like that. Such a size. He idly wondered if he could try and kill it on the return journey. After all, it had not moved easily. Perhaps it was injured.

He looked out onto the plain below. Yes, such a trophy as well as killing the wolves and children would make up for this nightmare. Now open countryside beckoned. They would catch them on the plains.

* * *

The next day the wolves continued their journey. They were in the foothills now. The wall. Yes, it was a wall they all agreed. Wolvzzar hoped they would be there by the end of the day. Perhaps they could then take a proper rest. Boy was exhausted after yesterday. His head ached still, his eyes stung. Yes, a day of rest would be so good if Wolvzzar would spare the time.

Boy felt too tired to be constantly on the watch for more monsters. He was relieved they had only seen animals from afar and heard cries so faint it could not mean danger for them. The hours were long and the mountain seemed to remain tantalizingly close but no closer.

"Boy." Mellana shouted in alarm. He jolted awake. "You were asleep. Are you okay Boy?" She rode up alongside him.

"Yes, just tired. I'll be fine." He clung on to Byter, lulled by the rhythm of his even pace. Suddenly he felt a sharp pain. He had been hit on the side and on his head. No, he was rolling. He was on the ground. His head ached. His side hurt. He opened his eyes, but it was such an effort. He tried to move.

"Boy." Byter bent down to him. "Are you injured? Have you broken anything?"

"Where are you hurt?" Mellana said.

"No. I'm ok I think. Must have slipped off." He blinked and closed his eyes again.

"You fell off, because you were asleep," she said checking the back of his head. "You haven't cut your head. No blood. Can you move your arms and legs?"

He nodded drifting away. "Can you hear me?" Mellana shook him gently.

"Boy." Wolvzzar's voice "You must focus. Open your eyes Boy." He obeyed and found those yellow and black eyes looking deep into his. Wolvzzar nodded, "I think you are just tired and need to rest. Yesterday was too much for you."

He came to a decision and addressed the pack.

"We are lucky to be by this small wood. We stay here for the day. Grapors, you and three others scout and guard for danger. Hunnta and Sylvabak search for food." A nod and they were gone. Boy closed his eyes. He would stay here for a moment. The grass was so comfortable and cool beneath him.

"Boy. Boy. It's time to wake up. How do you feel?"
It was Mellana. He felt strange. Thick headed. It was difficult to focus. The pack was restlessly moving about behind her. He couldn't see that well because it was dawn. Dawn! He looked up into her concerned face.

"How long have I been asleep?"

"Since yesterday afternoon," came the reply behind him. He looked behind him and there was Byter looking down at him. Boy was open mouthed.

"But that's not possible."

"We were getting worried. We could not wake you." Wolvzzar said. "You have been given an extraordinary gift. It is something only you can learn to use and control. But I think you must, like a young cub, learn to master walking before running."

Boy nodded, still amazed at how long he had been asleep.

"If you are well enough we will leave soon."

The other pack members were restlessly pacing and sniffing the air.

Mellana noticed their mood.

"Is there something wrong Byter?" she asked Byter. He looked at Wolvzzar who nodded.

"There is something out there. A new danger perhaps. We can't see or smell anything. But out there is something. We all feel it." He recovered his cheerfulness. "Come, Mellana has food for you, though why you would need food when you have done so little escapes me. Eat and drink quickly or we might leave you behind."

Boy grinned, realising he was seriously hungry. He thanked Mellana and took the food. In no time he had eaten and was astride Byter.

"See if you can stay up this time Boy. We have not travelled this far, to lose you now."

"Yes Byter, I will try," he laughed.

The day seemed to fly. The mountain was suddenly close. It reached up high, but its lower slopes were a gentle gradient. Snow at the top, then rock and below the rock trees, then grass and lastly grass and banks of the purple and yellow flowers. The richest of purple, broken up by fingers of yellow reaching up into the banks of purple.

* * *

The captain looked back in horror.

"By the Emperor's beard, what is it!! What kind of world is this! We cannot fight such a monster. It is huge. Yes, I know it is catching us Sergeant. Fool!"

The captain looked behind him again. It was getting too close.

"You there, release the spare horse. Let us hope it will follow it and be food enough for it. Now ride the rest of you, ride for your lives!"

* * *

The wolves ran and ran, seemingly determined to make up for the lost time. The wall could now be clearly seen, it was immense. Boy saw Wolvzzar swerve to the right. The line of wolves followed. He couldn't see why and then, he spotted it. A thin black vertical line, breaking up the grey wall. A gap or entrance perhaps?

Gradually the wall grew larger and more imposing. The black line was an entrance. They hurried towards it. Slowly and then more quickly he could make out the detail.
The wall, made up of massive stone blocks, was as high as any of the monsters they had seen. An impenetrable barrier.

It seemed hours before they stood before the entrance, or what was the entrance. It was blocked by rubble, that stretched up, nearly as high as the wall either side. Steep piles of rubble that no wolf could ever climb.

They all stood still, not talking, concentrating. There had to be a way. Set against each wall end was a column. Massive, thick. The two columns reach up to just above the wall. Their tops jagged. The rest had toppled into the entrance.

A statue, broken in the fall. It must have been huge. Only the shield it was carrying was intact. On its side a quarter of the way up. It had a crown with six stones carved into it.

Boy stopped still. Beside it, giant pieces of rubble leaning against each other. Between them, darkness. Tall and triangle shaped. A hole? A way through? It looked as though it might be just wide enough for the wolves to squeeze through but nothing bigger. The rubble up to it was less steep. A struggle, but perhaps could be reached by the pack. He turned excitedly to tell Wolvzzar but then realised he and the pack had also seen it and were moving towards it.

Hunnta led the way and with much slipping and cursing, hauled himself up to the gap. He stood quite still, looking through, ears twitching for every sound. Everyone watched. Boy could hear his own breathing in the silence. The large wolf turned and looked back down.

"I do not sense danger. There is day light at the other end. It is wide enough, although some of us may struggle."

Wolvzzar nodded to Smorlears, the slimmest of the pack. She scrambled up past Hunnta, sniffed the gap for a second and was gone. Silence.

"Smorlears, are you there?" Hunnta called out. "Answer me?"

A distant reply. "I am the other side. It is safe to come through."

The pack formed a queue to follow Wolvzzar up. He

and Hunnta struggled with the narrower parts but Mellana and Boy, were able to get through easily. The gap was a couple of metres deep with a very uneven floor so they had to be careful where they walked. They stepped out into the open air and were met by the sweetest of scents. It made them both smile and take in deep breathes to enjoy the rich perfume.

They took in the vision before them. A long tree lined avenue, the path made up of some kind of light coloured broad slabs of stone, now covered with grass and weeds that almost formed a complete carpet. The avenue led up to another small wall and ruined archway. Beyond it, the beginning of the slope up the mountain.

The trees were of normal height, which is why, Boy realised, they could not be seen from outside. There was a silence, an eerie silence about the place. Either side of the trees were lots of hillocks stretching out along the wall, as far as the eye could see. He walked slowly alongside the trees that lined the avenue. The hillocks. They were grassy but covering something. He realised with a shock, the hillocks were covering old buildings. Hundreds and hundreds of buildings. It was a ruined city.

He ran to Mellana. Together they walked up the avenue, looking curiously to either side of them. They stepped through the archway and were joined by the wolves. They all stood, speechless and utterly still. It was the fields of yellow and purple.

Byter came up beside him and recited the Prophesy.

'Seek a mountain of yellow and purple
though creatures terrible to see.'

"We have made it Boy. We have finally arrived."
Wolvzzar continued the next lines.

'Harvest the goodness that grows there
To save those at home who may die.

Yet only one on two legs can help you,
and only one who carries our sign.'

"We must hurry Boy. I do not think we have that long."
Boy, felt his stomach lurch.
"Do what Wolvzzar. I don't know what to do?"
He looked at the banks of flowers. The purple, layers of large petals, a bit like a rose. The yellow with three small flowers, swayed in the gentle breeze.
There was a silence, then Mellana spoke up.
"Perhaps Boy, we need to pick or crush the plants, like the healers do."
Boy turned around to face her. He could feel himself begin to panic.
"How and with what?"
He whirled round to Wolvzzar. "I'm sorry I have never done anything with plants. Ever. Mum and Dad looked after the garden at home."
Wolvzzar came up to them both.
"Then we must try. You are the Prophesy, there will be a way. Mellana, let us start with your idea."

She half-smiled and looked around. They were on a flat semi-circle of ground cut into the slope. Whilst the pack lay down on the surrounding slope, she reached into the basket and fetched out the leaf bowl she used for eating and a knife. She cut some of the flowers at the base of their stems and explained to Boy.

"I'm going to see if I can crush them to release the juice." She looked up at Boy, serious, but calm. He took heart from her and began to feel hopeful.

"Yes, perhaps that's it. The juice."
He had no idea. He couldn't think, but trusted Mellana. She would find the answer for them. She took a flat stone and crushed the flowers against the sides of the bowl. They became crushed but that was all.

"Perhaps I should boil them." She announced. She collected wood, whilst Boy and Byter sought a stream. By the time they came back Mellana had a fire going. She put more of the flowers into water. Whilst they waited Boy tried to distract himself by asking questions.

"Byter? Who built these walls and these buildings? Do you think it was the same people who built the tunnel and the steps?"

"I do not know Boy." He looked around. "It is a strange place. I think there are many stories here to tell."
The tension around the camp was growing. The wolves were prowling around. Boy stood and sat but couldn't remain still.

Mellana squinted up at him, "Boy, I shall scream if you don't sit down and keep still."

"Yes, but what if it doesn't work. The colour hasn't changed!"

She looked up at him, frowning. The worry, clear on her face.

"It might be a flavour. We will have to wait. Please Boy."

He immediately sat, willing himself to be calm.

"I'm sorry Mellana. Yes, you are right. Do you think it is ready yet?"

She sighed and hunched her shoulders.

"Let's wait a bit longer, shall we."

Byter lay down beside them. "Perhaps Mellana is right Boy. We have travelled this long, a little while longer won't hurt."

He nodded his agreement but secretly wanted them to have agreed to taste it then. They sat, saying nothing, just watching the bowl and flames.

It was late afternoon. Mellana looked up at Boy and Byter, half-smiled and taking took a spoon, blew on the scalding water and then sipped it. He became aware that the pack had gathered around them. All were watching her. She sat still, concentrating on the taste of the liquid in her mouth.

Boy looked at her expectantly, heart in his mouth. He willed it to be the answer. Just when he thought he would burst with tension, she frowned, sipped it again and finally turned to Boy and Wolvzzar.

"I can't taste anything. It tastes of just water. The water hasn't changed colour either. I don't think anything has happened. Boiling it doesn't work Boy. I'm sorry, but I don't think I can do anything."

She grimaced and leaned towards Boy, her face full of sympathy and concern.

"I'm not really part of the Prophesy. I think it must be you somehow Boy. After all, all the other parts have come true, haven't they?"

Boy felt frustration and panic.

"Yes, but this is different! I don't know anything about plants and stuff do I."

"But you didn't know how to walk through a wall or make a huge bird burst into flames or make a herd of giant animals follow and protect you. You knew none of it. So why don't you sit and here, take these plants and just try."

She held the plants out to him. He felt the pack's eyes on him.

Boy took the proffered yellow and purple plants. He took a deep breath. He held them in his palms and looked at them. He stared at the plants. He concentrated, willing it to do something, to make something happen inside him or to the plants. But nothing.

The wolves waited patiently as the sun set and darkness spread around them. Boy felt more and more helpless. He had stared and stared. He had closed his eyes and willed it. He had stroked the bunch, crushed it, pleaded with it. Ordered it. But nothing. No 'goodness'.

"I don't even know what the 'goodness' is?" he exclaimed in exasperation to Mellana. She looked across at Boy. He was hunched up. Knees firmly against his chest, holding himself tightly, hands digging into his bare upper arms, head resting on his arms.

"I don't know the answer Boy." She looked up. The moon had risen. "Perhaps," she sighed, "perhaps you should try again tomorrow."

He looked up at the moon in his frustration. He sighed and angrily grabbed the last bunch of flowers that Mellana had cut for him in both hands and held them up in front of him.

"Why won't you release your, whatever it is!" He threw the flowers down and dropped his hands into his lap.

He stopped. His right hand, no both now, were tingling. He felt it move up his arms and through his body. He looked at his right hand. It felt odd. It was glistening in the moon light. He gasped and looked at Mellana with astonishment. He held out his hand to her.

"It's wet." He looked round for Byter. "Byter it's wet." He rushed to the fire and yes, he could clearly see it was wet. Mellana picked up the flowers and felt the base of the stems.

"He's right. Look! The goodness! It coming out of the stems. He's done it. Boy you've done it! I knew you would." She grinned and ran up and hugged him.

"Quickly", he said. "I need the bottle and lots and lots of flowers and yes you are right, the bowl, I need the bowl to start with." He couldn't believe it. It had happened. He was going to do it!

He looked around at the wolves, grinning broadly. The wolves were all giving their congratulations, pacing around the edge, as excited at the children, but fearful of getting in the way.

Mellana quickly cut some flowers at the base of their stems as before, whilst Boy set up the bowl in front of him. He sat down taking the fresh bunch from Mellana and suddenly felt a pang of doubt. After all, he had no idea what he done earlier, only that he had done it. Heart in mouth, he held the stems over the bowl and squeezed. Nothing. The tingling was there, but not as strong. He felt the panic rising again, he squeezed harder. Nothing. Mellana bent down.

"The flower Boy, squeeze the flower heads."

Boy nodded and took the heads in his hands and crushed them. Nothing. But the power. The tingling. It was stronger again. Then, his heart stopped. A drop, another, another, a gentle flow. It was working. He looked up, felt the relief flow through him. Excited he took another and then another bunch. It was working. The power and tingling were there. The juice flowed freely. He couldn't see the colour and didn't care. It was working.

The wolves bayed and bayed. He and Mellana laughed at the wolves' song of joy. They laughed as they worked. The relief. He had done it. No, they had done it.

Chapter 17 - Time to Return

The Captain sat exhausted on the ground. His horse, head hung down, shivered beside him. He had never known such a day. The creatures. He shook his head. No one would believe him when he retold his story at home. He looked around. The soldiers, just lay where they got off or fell off their horses. Prime troops. The best there was, reduced to this. He looked up at the mountain. Why had the wolves risked this? What had driven them? He lay back. What prize could be worth this?

* * *

It was nearly dawn by the time the bottle was full. Boy was exhausted but elated.

"Do you think that will be enough Byter?"

The wolf looked at the bottle. "We cannot know. We can only hope."

Mellana was in the process of unpacking the two baskets that had carried essentials for her and Boy. Each was now only half full anyway, but she made room, so they could carry as many flowers back as possible, just in case they were needed.

"We do not know if there is enough goodness in the bottle, we do not know if the goodness in the flowers will dry up, but too much is at stake. If there is not enough, then perhaps Boy, you can make some more."

Although Boy was tired, he was eager to start the journey home. They all agreed that they would set out that morning and so hurried to pack up and begin.

Byter and Boy led the way whilst Wolvzzar checked the basket with the bottle with Mellana one last time. They almost strolled down the avenue, the morning sun warming them.

"Will you return to your home Boy, when we are back at the village?"

"Yes Byter, but I shall miss you all. Perhaps I might be able to come back. That would be the best." He smiled at the thought of returning at weekends, when he was staying with Gramdi.

They climbed the broken stones by the entrance and looked back at the mountain. Boy sighed, he knew a long and dangerous journey awaited. The happy relaxed thoughts disappeared and the knot of tension returned as he started to think about the dangers outside.

He climbed up the rubble, pushed through the gap, feeling the jagged stones brushing his arm as he carefully stepped his way over the broken floor and through to the other side.

Suddenly there were hands gripping him. Hurting his arms. He was being hauled through the gap. He tripped on the rubble strewn floor. He was picked up by a man in tattered tunic. He looked angry. He was covered in dirt and dust. There were other men with spears. It was so confusing. He shouted for Byter. The wolves were baying, there were men shouting and there was a crunching noise. He turned his head. They were rolling the massive stone shield across the gap before Byter could get through.

Boy desperately squirmed against the hands to get away. He could see Byter over the top of the round shield, but his snarling and growls and efforts to push against it were useless. The hands hurt his arms even more as he was roughly pulled round. A hand gripped his chin and forced him to look up. Into the sneering face of his captor. He tried to make sense of it.

Boy felt fear wash through him. He couldn't understand what was happening. Men with swords and spears. Why were they holding him? What were they going to do to him?

"And what do we have here. A village child. The captain is going to enjoy this. Where do you want the brat, Captain?"

Another man, beside the rolled stone shield that blocked the entrance, was laughing at Byter's increasingly desperate efforts. A sword and knife hung from his waist.

He looked round. Boy felt a cold dread through him.

"*Boy, are you there? Are you safe?*" It was Wolvzzar's voice in his head.

Before he could answer, the man walked towards him. He was probably in his thirties; his face was cold and hard. He looked Boy up and down before grabbing Boy by his tunic.

"Men have died chasing you. My men. You will pay for that. Now why are you here and what is behind there that is so important?"

He threw Boy to the floor. Shock and pain hit him. He had never been so frightened in his life.

"*Wolvzzar,*" said Boy in his mind. "*There are men with swords. They say they will kill me. They want to know why we are here. What am I to do Wolvzzar? Who are they? I've never seen them before.*"

"*Calm Boy calm. Tell me what you see. Take deep breaths and look and tell me.*"

"Captain, if we climb up the ruins, we can throw our spears down and kill them from above."
The Captain looked up at a soldier who had climbed on to the very top of the broken archway.

"Well done Sergeant. This I like. Finally, a useful suggestion. I will deal with this brat first. Then we can gather the men up there with you. I am going to enjoy this." He turned to Boy. "You can save them lad. Tell me what you are doing here and we will not kill the pack. Well?"

Boy knew he was lying. He was telling Wolvzzar what was happening and being said. It helped keep the panic at bay.

"*There must be fifteen of them Wolvzzar. All with swords and spears. They are mostly on the ground by the entrance. There are two with me and the Captain and one on the top. He is saying they will throw their spears down onto you.*"

"*We see him. You must tell them the truth Boy. These men will know if you are lying. It does not matter now if they know or not.*"

He felt the power beginning to build in him, but he knew somehow, it could not work against this man. Not yet.

There was something else though. All such thoughts disappeared as the man who they called Captain kicked Boy with his foot.

"Well village brat? What have you to say?"

Before he could speak, there was a cry from the top of the archway.

"Captain." Boy looked up as well. The Sergeant was pointing into the distance. Two men beside him were shielding their eyes.

"Well," said the Captain, "what is it?"

"On the horizon. Dust. Like a troop of men. It's coming straight towards us I think. I can only see one shape though. Doesn't make sense."

The Captain stood beside Boy and watched. Boy could see from the frown on his face he was concerned. He grabbed Boy's arm.

"Do you know what it is?" And turned him so he could see the dust. But the sun was still close to the horizon. It shone in his eyes.

"I don't know Sir. It's not any of us."

"I think it's just one thing," said one of the men. "It must be big."

Suddenly Boy was forgotten. The Captain sprang further up the stones so he could see better.

"Sergeant, is it any clearer?"

Wolvzzar had told the wolves to stay where they were, at the blocked gap. He did not want the soldiers to act in haste and start throwing down their spears.

Boy was left alone on the ground. He could feel the power growing now. *It must be a beast,* he thought.

"Come to me," he whispered to it. "Quickly! Come to me." He looked around. There were plenty of hiding places he could crawl into if necessary.

"*Stay still, but be prepared to run. Byter can see it, he thinks it is one animal.*"

Wolvzzar told the pack to slowly back out and form a semi-circle around the back of the entrance, to stop the soldiers coming over the top.

There was a tense silence, as the men watched the cloud get nearer, the shape begin to take form. The men began to get alarmed as they too realised it was a single thing. A big thing.

Boy heard neighing. Horses. He hadn't seen them before. The men's horses were tied up further along the wall. They were getting agitated, pulling against their tethers.

"It's the thing, the monster. That creature that chased us!" shouted one man.

"Captain what do we do?" shouted another.

"It's the monster, isn't it Captain," the Sergeant exclaimed. "It's followed us."

"It's going to kill us all this time." A new voice. A whine almost. They were all shouting, moving around, looking for places to hide in the rocks.

The Captain stood there, hands on hips, lips tightly drawn. watching.

"So close. So close to winning," he whispered to himself. He looked at his men and then back to the approaching shape. Boy did not know what he was thinking, but instinctively knew he had to hide. The men were shouting, the horses were screaming wildly and trying to get away.

"You. Grab the brat. The rest of you up here," The Captain ordered. But before any could move, Boy was off and running across the broken archway to a small hole under the fallen column and amongst the huge scattered stones. It was small. Only he or Mellana could have squeezed into the opening. He felt the jagged stones scraping his arms and legs but he was in. It was bigger inside. He could see it was L shaped. He twisted round the 'L' shape so he could look out, but could not be reached.

Scrabbling outside, footsteps on loose stones. A curse and a dirty hand and leather covered arm were waving around, fingers searching for him. He pushed himself up against the side wall, legs against his chest, holding his breath. He dared not move. His heart pounded. The dirty hand moved around, felt the edge of the wall, where it turned and hid Boy. Stones moving. Then the hand had gone. Boy stared at the entrance watching and waiting. He strained to hear every sound. The background noise of neighing and shouts of men, but close to him, heavy breathing and grunts of effort. Then the arm and hand were back.

"I know you are there you little brat. Wait till I get you. I'll teach you."

The hand reached the corner. Grunting as the arm changed angles. The hand came again, further round. Despite the man mostly blocking the entrance, Boy could see his hand. There were small chips of stone beside him. One shaped like a triangle, a knife. He picked it up and jabbed it at the hand. A scream and the hand was gone. More cursing. A whine almost.

"By his crown it's coming, coming. You little toad. You'll pay. Do you hear me. You'll pay for this."

Then a scrape of metal and wood. Boy jerked back, banged head against the wall and winced. It was a spear. The man grunted, then the spear jerked forward. Back and forward again and again at different angles. It was near his face. It was gone. It scraped against the side of the entrance. He couldn't get it round any further. It dropped down, back again near his ankles. He hugged himself as tightly as he could. He hardly dared breathe. More curses.

"Can't reach him. I'm coming up. It's the monster for sure." Then footsteps running away.

He edged round carefully and looked out of his hiding place. He could see the men climbing up or milling around near the top of the fallen archway. The one who had tried to spear Boy, was climbing as quickly as he could to join the others. They were all looking around for places to hide.

"Get over that wall and finish those wolves," the Captain screamed at them. They all started to climb up the rubble as quickly as they could, slipping in their panic, looking over their shoulders at the advancing dust cloud. The wolves were barking and baying. The ground was beginning to rumble.

"Faster," Boy called. "Faster."

The rumble became thumps. He could hear its roar.

"Steady," said Wolvzzar. *"Watch if any try and throw their spears. We do not want to give them a chance to re-group on the flat ground. Take them on the stones as they come over."*

A roar, an ear-piercing roar. The ground trembled with each step and a huge shadow cut across the ground in front of Boy. The horses were screaming in the background, men shouted in terror and then there it was, the giant two-legged predator, towering over the soldiers.

It was massive. Not as tall as the wall, Boy could see its back long tail, huge legs and beak like mouth. It leaned down towards the man who had tried to get Boy. It knocked his spear to one side and opened its huge beak. The man threw up his arms to protect himself, he was grabbed and the limp form thrown onto the ruined archway. The creature turned, started to climb up the rubble. Its head came down, another man gone. Too late to climb over the rubble, the soldiers desperately tried to hide amongst the broken boulders. It sought them out, one after another. It climbed to the blocked gap.

Wolvzzar's calm voice "A soldier is coming down. He going to attack. Watch his spear!" But the soldier was no match for Hunnta and was quickly dispatched.

A final whinny from the horses, they had broken away. They were running as fast as they could back over the plains. Boy smiled. A roar from the monster. It was looking around for any more men. Its huge feet searched for purchase, sliding and pulling the stones down as it looked around the top of the fallen archway. It leaned down near the top once again. And then all was quiet, the soldiers were no more.

The beast could not climb higher, it was too steep. It could look over the top, but no more. It roared as it looked down at the wolf pack on the other side.

"Stay still pack. Do not move," ordered Wolvzzar.
Boy had moved forward and was squatting by the entrance. He stood up, feeling the power course through him.

"Stop!" he ordered as he raised his hands. "Stop!" he shouted again. It turned and stared at Boy roaring defiance. "Go now."
He felt the beast's resistance. He concentrated more. Felt this time a tingling in his arms, as though the power were almost physical, leaving him through his arms. He pointed at the Beast.
"Go!"

The creature roared at him in defiance but he felt its resistance diminishing. It turned and started to climb down. It was watching him through a single tiny eye as it started to move away from the archway. Boy had to look up and up to retain control as it neared him. He felt the power of the beast, smelt the strong animal scent, he almost wavered. He did not dare take his eyes away from the beast's eye.

It turned its head towards him, beginning to bend down. The huge claws on its powerful front legs closer. It opened its huge beak, showing the deadly rows of yellow teeth along its mouth and then a final roar. The noise was deafening, the breath hot and rank. It made him blink for a second. But the beast was turning away. It stood up and carried on past. The ground shook as it strode into the distance.

Chapter 18 - The Journey Home

A bark. Boy looked up and grinned. In its efforts to reach the soldiers, the beast had dislodged the stone shield blocking the gap. The wolves were streaming down. They surrounded him. He hugged them as they licked his face, swirling around him. He was laughing for joy. Then he felt Mellana's arms around him, hugging him and he was hugging her back.

"You do look a sight," said Byter, "but I'm glad to see you've got nothing more than a few cuts and bruises."
Boy dusted himself down laughing and reassuring them the cuts did not hurt.

"Well done Boy. You are indeed the Prophesy."
Wolvzzar gathered the pack around him. He spoke of the journey back, the need for care and caution. But there was a lightness about them all as they faced whatever lay ahead. Boy knew it was because he was there. He had proved that he could and would protect them. Not to hurt other animals, just to stop them hurting the pack. His pack.

And so they set off. It became a time of routines. Strange routines. Scouts spotting the giant creatures, Boy gently encouraging them to move away from the pack. His strength grew and he was able to better focus his thoughts, engage with animals further away, keeping them at a safe distance.

Very soon the mountains of the East began to take shape and then a green band around their base. A band that became a forest, the jungle that would lead to the steps, the tunnel and the land of the Kith of Chylgar.

* * *

The Captain had watched them leave. He ached all over. He stretched and looked out over the plain. He had been right to keep the injured soldier and not leave him, when he had been hurt in the jungle by the big cat. He had proved useful after all. The beast had killed him and thrown him on top of the Captain. He had survived.

He thanked the man as he kicked the body over the edge. He had remained hidden amongst the stones until he felt sure the pack had gone. He nodded to himself. There was his horse, patiently waiting, a stray beside it.

He would return home safely and he would return a hero. The fact the pack had escaped him would be nothing. For he had discovered the Lost City. He smiled and looked at the broken columns. There could be no mistake. The legend of the City and the Crown of Power. It was real after all. It was here and he had found it. The Emperor would reward him with anything he asked.

The boy though. He had power. Real power. He had watched through a gap in the stones, amazed as the boy had controlled the giant killer. He should have killed him when he had the chance. The Warlocks would need to be told. He grimaced.

They were not to be trusted, but they would be needed.

* * *

They entered the jungle with a sense of dread. The heat, the closeness, so many dangers they could not see or did not understand.

It was the morning of the second day that the Wolves became restless. Neither Mellana or Boy had felt anything, but both knew to trust the packs instincts. They ran together as closely as they could, on their guard every minute. Time and again Byter jerked to the left or right, convinced he had seen something. They lay that night exhausted.

"I know I smelt something. It was only for a second. I have had that scent in my nostrils before," said Hunnta.

"You are right," said Growler. "There is a stillness in the air this time. It is too quiet. When we entered the jungle before, there was such a noise. I had never heard such a calling of animals and birds screaming and singing. Yet this time..." They all listened.

"You are right," Wolvzzar reflected. "There is only birdsong. There is a predator here. One that moves on the ground, perhaps of the size and strength of the giant cat. Or indeed the Cat itself."

The next day, it was the same. The wolves became increasingly nervous. Stopping time and again. Once Hunnta, who was scouting in front, came rushing back.

"It is him! The Cat. I am sure of it," said Hunnta breathlessly. "I only caught a glimpse for a second. But I am sure it was him."

"Be on your guard everyone." Wolvzzar warned. "We must keep moving."

Evening brought them to a clearing. As big as the one where Boy had faced the giant cat. A stream ran near the far edge. They walked exhausted across the clearing and quenched their thirsts before lying down by the jungle edge. Bird song, insects buzzing, but there was no other sound. Wolvzzar remained standing, sniffing the air.

"What is it Wolvzzar?" Mellana asked.

"I sense a power. Across the clearing. Be still everyone." The bushes and lower branches were moving. A face. Then a head and then the body, of the giant cat. It paused, looked at them and sat on its haunches.

It was even bigger than Boy remembered. Over two metres of muscled strength. As broad as Byter and Growler put together. It looked at Boy and a voice came into his head.

"*You have done well child, but have a care, you still have much to learn. I am in your debt. It shall be repaid now. You shall be safe here.*" With that, he looked about the clearing in a slow deliberate manner. He closed his eyes once and then stood, turned around and was gone.

The pack looked to Wolvzzar who spoke before they could.

"He talked to Boy, but this time I could hear. He offers protection. In payment of the debt," nodding towards Boy. "I for one will sleep much easier knowing he is there protecting us. I suggest we all get some sleep, dawn is not far behind us."

"Are you sure?" said Hunnta. "Can we trust it?"

"Yes Hunnta, we can trust him. You would have been dead, many times over, had he chosen it. Rest easy all of you."

They made much greater progress through the rest of the jungle, no longer careful of every noise. Soon they reached the steps leading to the waterfall. Here Boy was alert, constantly watching the sky. He had found that he was able to call the power at will, so that when a bird began to come close, he ensured it quickly sheered away.

Soon they were on the plains again, days upon days of long rides and running. The pack and everyone had mixed feelings. Tired of the travel but relieved, because this was their Land, a land they could feel safe in. They were increasingly heartened by the sight of the Mountains of the North in the far distance, the slopes of which were their destination and home to the five packs. Wolvzzar pushed and pushed them.

"I fear time is short," he said one morning. "Mellana, I would ask that we bypass your village, we cannot afford to stop. If you wish, we will leave you near it so you can walk to your people?" But although Mellana had been counting the hours, she refused any thought of not carrying on with them to the home of the Northern packs.

For Boy though, this was the best of times. Time for talking with Mellana and Byter about the birds, animal and plants of the Land. A time to enjoy being fitter and feeling healthier. Of running without tiring. A time when he did not spend most of the day with his stomach knotted in fear.

The day of arrival should have been a joyous occasion. Boy had been watching the changes in the landscape with fascination. The mountains of the West were tall. But as nothing compared to these Northern mountains. Colossal peaks, that seemed to reach the sky, one after another. Impossibly sheer, stretching out as far as the eye could see.

Their camp was on the lower slopes, beside a wood and stream. A network of caves that had been the wolves' home since the beginning of the pack. He was looking forward to seeing where Byter lived.

It should have been a time of greeting and celebration with the full pack, a time to tell their tales and of course see their families. Yet the camp was silent when they arrived. It had proved too late for the oldest and youngest. Both Wolvzzar and Byter had lost relatives. Many of those that were left, had the sickness, were shrunken and clearly close to death. Wolves sat at the entrance to caves, too weak to rise and greet the wanderers.

Wolvzzar took them straight to the largest cave, a natural hall, where all the wolves could gather for the meetings, a place for all matters relating to the pack to be discussed. Wolvzzar was relieved that Mellana had stayed for he knew she would take care of dispensing the goodness. The basket was brought in for her. Now battered with many rips and the handle nearly eaten away where the wolves had carried it in their mouths. It was carefully unpacked to reveal the bottle containing the Goodness.

Boy was looking around the cave. It had a hole in the wall above the front entrance, letting in the light, but branches swayed above it, ensuring the wind and rain were still kept out. The walls of grey and light blue were dry. He was wondering if he would sleep there or in one of the other caves when

Mellana gave a cry, "It's gone!"

She held out the bottle, her face ashen.

"What do you mean child?" said Wolvzzar urgently. There were tears forming in her eyes. All the wolves were watching.

"It's empty, the bottle is empty." Boy felt as though he had been punched.

Growler came up and nuzzled her.

"Tell us more," he whispered.

She took a deep breath.

"The liquid has vanished. I don't know if it has leaked away." She felt the bottom of the bottle and put her hand on the floor of the basket. It was damp.

"But I have been so careful to carry it without banging or dropping it," said Runlong. The wolf looked around for support. "You all know this."

"We know you have. There is no blame. It could have happened at any time," said Wolvzzar. He sat down on his haunches. There was silence. No one spoke. He stood again.

"We still have the plants. Fetch them. Boy, we do not have any time to waste. We need you to try again."

Boy felt his stomach lurch as the others rushed about, fetching and untying the bundles of plants that had been carried from the Purple Mountain. A pile was laid on the floor in front of him. Mellana sat down beside him.

"They still look okay don't they Boy."

He just nodded, breathing deeply.

He was trying to calm his nerves. He placed the bowl that Mellana had retrieved from the basket, in front of him. He thought about how he had done it last time. He took a bunch of flowers, held the stems in his left hand, the flowers in his right and crushed the flowers. He waited a few seconds, waiting for the tingling in his hand, the sense of power to build within him. But there was nothing. He felt himself begin to panic. He touched the bottom of the stems, just in case. Nothing. Dry. Completely dry. He looked across at Mellana, who was biting her lip.

Her face suddenly lit up.

"The base of the stems. Mum always cuts them. Let me cut them like she does." She took a little off the bottom and gave them back to Boy. He looked at her and then went through the same ritual. Nothing. He looked at Wolvzzar, who was pacing the cave floor. He came back to Boy.

"There must be something different. Describe everything to me."

Boy did not argue. Between nervous breaths, he explained how he sat, how he held the plants. How he felt. Except now there was no power.

"Of course," said Mellana. "It's obvious. It was at night. The moon was out. We could hardly see."

Wolvzzar nodded. He did not sound convinced.

"Are you sure you were not feeling any power Boy?"

He looked up into Wolvzzar's worried face. He hated letting Wolvzzar, of all the pack, down. There were so many ill animals depending on him. He felt sick.

"No," he shrugged. "I feel, I feel nothing."

"Let us wait for tonight's moon and hope." He left them. Boy felt so miserable. He had let them down, but he couldn't think what it was that was different. He thought he could call upon this power when he wanted.

The next few hours were the longest. It had never taken so long for the sun to set and the moon to rise. Mellana sat with Boy. They rarely spoke. Occasionally Byter would join them, but nothing he said, could raise Boy's spirits. Growler came and sat by Mellana. She rested her head against the wolf, it somehow made Boy feel even more alone.

It was mid evening when Wolvzzar came back into the cave to fetch Boy. Mellana brought out the rest of the pots, whilst Boy carefully carried the flowers out into the moonlight. The pack gathered around him. There were more faces tonight as pack members who had stayed at home to care for the sick, joined them. He tried to stay focused. But he was sure this time, in the moonlight, it would work. It had to.

He picked up the flowers, in his left hand, placed the bowl, in front of him. A new bunch of flowers, just to be sure. Mellana had cut off the bottoms, in case it would help. He looked one final time at Mellana. They both took a deep breath as he placed his right hand around the flower petals and squeezed and then squeezed hard. The pack watched expectantly. Nothing. He felt nothing. No power. Just his heart racing. He touched the base of the stem. There must be a mistake he thought. How could this be?

"It's not happening Wolvzzar. I'm sorry, I don't know what to do. Perhaps the flowers are too old. Perhaps we have to go back." His heart sank as he said it. He knew it would be too late for many in the pack. One by one the wolves had dropped their heads and slunk away.

Wolvzzar came up to Boy. "You have tried and tried again. I can ask no more." Turning he walked slowly into the dark.

Byter remained and lay down beside him. "Let us stay here. In the moonlight you discovered your secret. Perhaps if we wait."

"For what Byter," interrupted Boy. "I don't know what to wait for." He sat there, suddenly feeling cold and alone. He put his knees up and hugged himself, his palm across the mark of the wolfs head. It tingled.

He suddenly froze. He looked across at Mellana.

"I forgot. I sat like this on the mountain. Then I did it. Then it worked."

Boy stared at his hand. "My hand Byter. It's tingling."

"The mark Boy. The hand you used to crush the flowers was covering the mark of our people."

He looked from Byter to Mellana. He could feel the tingling spread. The power. It was growing. It was happening.

"Quickly. Pass me the flowers." He took the flowers. He took a deep breath and concentrated every fibre of his being on the flowers. He followed his ritual but could not bear to touch the base.

Looking down, he held the flowers out. "Please Mellana, feel the bottom of the stem for me. Is it wet?"
She leant across and with shaking fingers touched the plant. Her face widened into the biggest smile.

"It's wet Boy, it's wet." She turned to Byter and showed him her hand, it was glistening in the moonlight.

"It worked! It worked!" he yelled, reaching for more flowers "The bowl. Quickly, the bowl."

Wolvzzar ran up to them. "Tell me it's true."
Boy just nodded. He knew he had to concentrate. He dared not lose the feeling and continue to press the flowers. Byter and Mellana excitedly explained then re-explained and explained again, as more and more wolves joined them. Boy looked up to see a sea of faces and bodies moving backwards and forwards with excitement.

Then gradually the voices died. Boy looked up. The wolves were parting. A wolf was slowly coming towards him, carrying its cub in its mouth. The cub was whimpering. The mother placed it in front of Boy.

"Please, help my son," she simply said. All the wolves were silent. None would deny her this last and only chance to save her cub.

Mellana took out a small bowl, dipped it into the liquid and put it in front of the cub. It had slunk to the ground, closed its eyes and put its head on its front paws.

"Drink it my son, drink it," the mother wolf whispered to her cub. The cub's nostrils switched, it slowly lifted its head and looked at the bowl. Mellana pushed it under its chin, tilting it so that the pup could lick the contents without moving. It licked the precious liquid once, then sank its head down again. Boy looked at Mellana and the mother, not daring to move.

Nothing stirred, the only sound the gentle movement of the trees branches in the wind. All waited. Then the cub opened its eyes. It stretched and slowly and shakily stood up. It wagged its tail and turned to lick its mothers face. The wolves erupted. They bayed, yelped and leapt around in sheer joy and relief. Many rushed off to tell their ailing nearest and dearest that there was hope after all.

Wolvzzar sank to the ground and closed his eyes.

"The Prophesy is fulfilled," he said to himself.

He opened his eyes and looked at Boy. Boy felt the warmth and gratitude wash over him, before Wolvzzar even spoke.

"Thank you, Boy." He simply said. "Thank you."

Mellana grinned at Boy and then became businesslike. She turned to Wolvzzar.

"Shall we take the bowl to the ones who most need it?"

"Yes, yes, you are right." Wolvzzar stood up. "Come. Give way everyone. Let her pass."

Immediately the wolves parted and Mellana concentrating on every step, carefully walked towards the caves where the sick and dying wolves lay.

Boy continued to crush the plants, until all the flowers had been used. Amid an endless stream of thanks and congratulations, he quietly rose, smiling and thanking them, to make his way to the cave and sleep.

Chapter 19 - The Tunnel Calls

It was early the next morning that Boy and Mellana were woken. The goodness was working. All the wolves that had been ailing, even those close to death, were showing signs of recovery.

Byter explained that the wolves from the other four packs, were keen to return to their homes to treat the sick there. Mellana was asked to split the goodness between them and whilst she busied herself, Hunnta, Sylvabak, Growler and the others said their goodbyes. Boy felt uncomfortable with the praise and thanks heaped upon him, but mostly sad that he was saying goodbye to such good friends. All too soon he was standing beside Mellana and Byter as the wolves set off for the journey home.

He and Mellana agreed it was time for them to go home as well. After the relief that the danger was over, he felt exhausted and homesick. Amid bays and wishes of good will to them both, Wolvzzar, Byter, Blakthrote and the two children set out. Blakthrote had offered to carry Mellana now that Growler had returned to his own caves.

It was days before they reached the village. They were met at the outskirts by the village leader Centra and the Seer Wolfrea. After a formal welcome to the wolves, there were hugs and tears from Mellana's parents, and a welcome hug from Detra who was fully recovered. Everyone was delighted to see them return and brought food and drink, more delicious than Boy remembered.

They all sat in the fields and listened as Wolvzzar through Wolfrea told the story of what had happened.

Increasingly the eyes of the villagers turned from puzzlement, to amazement and then admiration as Wolfrea relayed the tale. But Boy wasn't really listening. A worm of worry had begun on the journey. What if he couldn't get through the tunnel. Last time it had just happened. He walked through solid wood. He had assumed all this time he would be able to. What if he couldn't?

They were all disappointed and particularly Detra and Mellana, when Boy explained he needed to go home that night. The worm of doubt had grown and now he just had to know. But he was also sad, because he had no idea if he would see them again. Any of them.

Detra joined Mellana and the three wolves as they accompanied Boy to the tunnel. It seemed to take forever, but finally they stood before the wooden wall, set into the tunnel entrance. Boy turned and hugged the children and Byter before turning to Wolvzzar.

"Do you think I will be able to come back Wolvzzar?" All of them turned expectantly to the large wolf. The yellow and black eyes, full of kindness and wisdom looked down into his.

"We do not know Boy. But I sense a shift in the way of the Land. I sense a corruption. You are the Prophesy. I believe in your power and your strength. Your spirit is now weaved into the Land. Perhaps you will be needed again, indeed it may well be that you return."

After final hugs to his friends. He faced the wooden wall. His breathing felt jagged, nervous. He was almost too afraid to touch it. He placed his hand upon it. Felt the cold, old wood against his palm and pushed. Nothing. His eyes focused on the wood, he concentrated hard willing a surge of power. Same again. Nothing. No give. He felt a rising panic when he heard Wolvzzar's voice.

"The sign Boy. Place your hand on your arm. It is the strength of all the packs. Of this I am now sure."

He placed his hand against the mark of the wolf on his arm. Rested it there. He glanced behind and saw the looks of encouragement on their faces. He closed his eyes and placed his hand on the wood. But there was nothing there. He opened his eyes quickly. His hand had gone. Only his wrist was visible. He grinned at them all and then pushed.

The same cold and damp cobwebby feeling as before, as he pushed through the wood. And then he was in the tunnel. The light was brighter this time, the swirling mist more billowing. He searched for and found the wall. He felt the wind suddenly pushing him, the mist clearing, the light going. He felt strange, his skin itchy. The air was cold and his clothes felt heavy. He was not unwell, but everything was somehow a bit of an effort.

Boy stretched. Something was odd. He reached the entrance and sighed with relief. There in front of him, in the moonlight, were the dim shapes of the garden. He walked out of the tunnel and towards the welcoming light of the kitchen window. He could see Gramdi moving around, busy as ever. He was home.

He hesitated and put his hands to his chest. His clothing. The wonderful tunic had gone. The heavy winter coat back. He looked down, his trainers, undamaged. He felt his tummy. It was back too. He grimaced. He would do something about that, he thought, as he walked towards the lovely cooking smells. But first he had quite a lot to tell Gramdi.

* * *

The Captain's face was thin, his clothing covered in dirt. Now with a gash down his chin, still red and angry, though healing.

He gazed out from the tunnel entrance across the land. Such a journey back. Twice the moon had risen and fallen before he had reached the tunnel that would take him through the mountains, to the Emperor and safety. Two days before, he had skirted the pack's caves. The wolves had looked healthy. Whatever it was they had found in the Purple Mountains, had clearly worked.

He shrugged. They had won the battle, but their victory would be short lived. For he would return and with him, Warlocks and an army that would conquer all.

The End

Also available from Simon Taylor

Imogen and Roari the Dragon

A story for 3-year-olds and above.

An enchanting story about eight-year old Imogen and her unexpected visitor, Roari the Dragon.

Beautifully illustrated, this first story describes how Imogen 'calls' Roari from another land and how together, they fly off in search of Scratch, a lost puppy.

Imogen and Roari the dragon go to the seaside

A story for children 3 - 8 years old

This is the second book in the series about Imogen and her best friend, Roari the dragon.

Imogen is sad because she has never been to the seaside. Can Roari help?

The delightfully illustrated story brings to life this magical tale as once again Imogen and Roari fly off on another big adventure.

Imogen and the Children from Undurbedd

A story for 7-year olds and above.

Imogen's best friend is a four-metre-tall dragon called Roari.

One night, she finds two tiny children in her bedroom who live in the land called Undurbedd.

They become friends and she visits their Land. But all is not well there and she and the two children, must fly with Roari on a journey to save their world from destruction.

A story of magic and adventure

Order on line today from www.simontaylorstoryteller.com